REFLECTIONS III

- in words an fantasy images

George Manus

2.edition

Author: George Manus
Copyright: George Manus
Design and layout: Ole Praud
Vignettes: Morten Løfberg
Copyright Fantasy images and cover: Jan Arnt

Print: BoD - Books on Demand, Norderstedt, Germany
Editor: BoD - Books on Demand, Copenhagen, Denmark (BoD.dk)
e-mail: george.manus@maxmanus.com

Other books written by George Manus:

THOUGHTS, English
TANKER, Norwegian

REFLECTIONS I, English
REFLEKSJONER I, Norwegian

REFLECTIONS II, English
REFLEKSJONER II, Norwegian

REFLEKSJONER III, Norwegian

A WOMAN'S MANY MIGRATIONS, English
EN KVINNES MANGE FLYTTINGER, Norwegian

INNOVATIONS AND CREATIONS, English

70 YEARS IN COMMUNICATION - about the MAX MANUS Companies, English
70 ÅR I KOMMUNIKASJON - om MAX MANUS firmaene, Norwegian

2018
ISBN: 9788743000747

Foreword

These "REFLECTIONS III" are dedicated to my wife Marianne which I married in 1998.

I have always been aware that I generally have a verbose expression. As long as I can remember I have always used more words than maybe necessary, to make sure that my message has been perceived. The reason may be related to my simpler form of dyslexia which unconsciously has to be compensated for? Everything I have written have been translated to English, the language we daily use for communication.

I don't believe my wife have read much of it, but she has clearly made heard her opinion.

"I write the way I behave in life, she says. For that reason it's impossible for me to solve problems in a simple way. I always chose the complicated route".

Maybe not very flattering but probably partly right.

As mentioned I have a verbose expression, for many being <u>too</u> complex. That it, after her opinion influences my ability to solve what I call challenges, not problems, must remain her problem.

Critic is important, and this one came after I kindly asked her to read through my translation of the reflection "Truth", to English. Probably one of the most complex.

I thank her for the tips and not the least for her patience related to my writings, which logically, now as it has come to seven books has taken much time and focusing.

My "Stories" often happened long time ago and as a consequence I can not guarantee the correctness of details and time-settings.

The "Reflections" on the other hand are subjective and therefore can not be used as valid references beyond my perception at the moment.

What's then the purpose of having written these "REFLECTION III"?

The answer must be as for my earlier writings, that I first and foremost write for myself. However, it would of course be a positive bonus if others could find pleasure in reading them

As before, I thank Anne Schild for her help with the language, Morten Løfberg for his vignettes, Jan Arnt for the front cover and his fantasy images, and my friend Ole Praud for his consultancy work.

2018
George Manus
george.manus@maxmanus.com

Application

May 2006

Application can be seen as a one-way motorway, which runs in a straight line towards a set destination in the distance, without this destination having been clearly defined. A definition of detail made at the beginning will end up being outdistanced as far as quality goes by the time the application is finished, which is only natural as the time factor "application time" has caused new requirements to be made and technology, as well as marketing conditions and other factors may have changed.

An example of an application: "A dictation system based on a communications system" already existing.

The product team, consisting of the best to be had both technically and commercially, specify the goal to a reasonable degree of detail.

The commercial requirements are given priority in the specification.

Then general fundamental guidelines are assessed as to which measures might lead to the goal.

To the extent possible, the necessary capacity requirements and time aspects are assessed; thus allowing the economic requirements to be measured as far as the application goes.

Knowing full well that it is impossible to find 100% accurate guidelines leading to the goal, based on where one happens to be at the time, an assessment of possible alternatives and an approach, on which the powers that be in management can base their decisions, is made anyway.

Alternatives are chosen or revised objectives are set up.

If it's shown that the application for practical reasons isn't feasible, the project is shelved.

It can, of course, happen that the idea is tossed around several times during this stage, for clarification and understanding.

We assume that the process is under way:

On all motorways there are exits to service stations, where one stops to check that everything is OK before filling one's tank and continuing.

Application work of all types is laid out with temporary goals along the way, so that one can exit at the service stations to test product status and market.

In bigger projects, bits of products, with a "there and then status", may be released to a special market for testing. This must only happen when the market accepts the status as is.

Feedback and experience provide the basis for re-entry onto the motorway with the final objective of getting across the finishing line as number one without having exceeded the speed limit.

The process is often repeated several times. The number of service stops depends on the team of participants and is determined by need and strategy.

In development context each service stop signifies a positive experience, giving one a constant idea of how the final product will be.

Perhaps one also achieves a sort of bonus in the form of economic opportunities from the part releases.

If the commercial and technical staff cooperate closely and well, the product keeps improving throughout the entire process and the product status which lies two-thirds or three-quarter into the race, may even surpass the product objective envisioned initially.

Attack is the best defence

March 2017

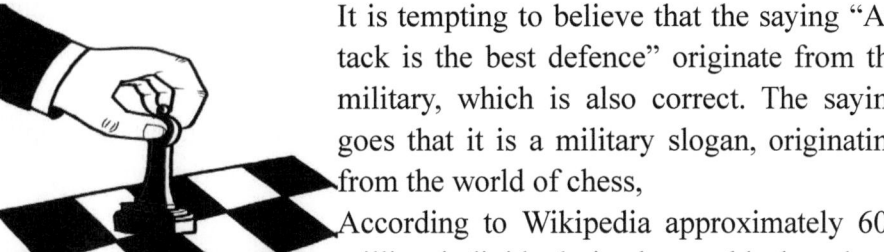

It is tempting to believe that the saying "Attack is the best defence" originate from the military, which is also correct. The saying goes that it is a military slogan, originating from the world of chess,

According to Wikipedia approximately 600 million individuals in the world play chess. Furthermore, it's said that chess was plaid already before year 600.

Despite that being long ago, people started wars infinity before that. Yeas, all the way back to the time when Adam and Eve started the procreation of us humans so we could get on with quarrelling.

The more people the more diversified opinions and thereby excuses for disagreeing.

Everything needs development, so maybe thanks to the chess we got more system into the quarrelling and warlike madness.

To me this sounds logical.

I don't play chess but understand that the objective is to put the King out of play.

Present days the Kings and the Queens normally have limited power, and that apart, we as well have a lot of other forms of governance than the Royalty.

This said, it must be added that there still are Kings and Queen around the world with unlimited power, and where they could well make use of a little democracy.

Well, the analogy fails little. Maybe undemocratic according to today's existing perceptions, that in the word of chess only the King can be chess mate. Not the Queen.

To put any form of governance out of play, the attacker needs good strategy and tactics, and chess is, I understand a game where it is prerequisite that one can handle these areas.

Many moves must be planned before both horses, knights, farmers and others can be put in motion with the aim to crush the leader of the opposition.

The final aim is to put the opposition, the King, under chess mate, but a game can also end with remis, explained as equal. Furthermore, a game of chess can also be won by one of the parties surrendering.

Already back in the 50th, data machines where programmed to play chess and in 1997 the Deep Blue machine became the first winning over the world champion in chess.

Apparently, today it is easy for the machine to win, something I gather is a result of their ability to attack in such way that it becomes the best defence.

I wonder if one in modern warfare uses data controlled attack and defence models, but take that for granted.

I am a believer of finding more sympathetic ways to defend oneself than to be the attacker, but the question is, does it have the same effect.

This is where personality comes at hand.

It seems to be somewhat primitive about having to attack to defend oneself but nothing is black or white, not even in this context.

Faced with an violent attacker it is only reasonable that one have to defend oneself with all means available to avoid being a victim - in other words attack to defend oneself.

An attack may not necessarily be of physical nature.

It's well known, and I personally know quite a few not violent persons, who daily use to attack first, after their opinion to obtain an upper hand in the beginning of a discussion. Such an attack often brings an immediate defence for the one, as the attacked easily is brought off balance. On the other hand, if the attack seems irrational, the defence become strengthened as the attacked will have difficulties immediately to find rational counter-arguments.

People with these characteristics, attacking first in the believe it's the best defence are normally not very sympathetic, but this of course becomes subjective from my side.

It can also be questioned if this is a characteristic one eventually is born with, or if it is taught by experience in daily practical life.

I can't let this chance pass. I add what to me must be the best actual example for this saying still to be practiced.

Among others, maybe it is through extensive practicing of this saying that Donald Trump did find his way to the White House after becoming President number 45 in USA?

I doubt that most of us are so conscious that we plan to attack first to strengthen our defence.

I rather believe that most of us in the daily life will chose a balanced approach adapted to the actual situation one encounter. That way everything will become milder.

I don't invite to further polemic around this subject. Each and one of us must make up their opinion about if it's right that: Attack is the best defence.

Capacity utilization and insidious development

April 1999

In the mountainous country, up North, it once upon a time was a development department with limited capacity in relation to the tasks they were engaged in.

Having many assignments was of course positive, but the limited capacity often led to the fact that completions often became delayed according to expectations from the commercial side.

It wasn't only just to extend the capacity, as it had both to do with economy and time.

To extend the capacity would also require training, which in short term would drain capacity in the small environment in the development department.

At a point in time, really long after one should have done it, with the back against the wall when it came to assignments, one finally took the decision to extend the capacity, and as predicted, valuable capacity was lost due to training.

Everyone agreed that extension of the capacity was needed, and a must to be able to advance on longer terms, but the pressure on the developers just increased.

Worst of all, from the moment of the extension, one of the developers had to assist the sales department in larger and important customer presentations. One agreed that this direct customer contact was valuable for his self-development, but then what about his capacity to perform development?

The companies' products increased in popularity and market share, the one project after the other popped up, and the greater success the greater demand for technical assistance in customer presentations.

The general consensus was that the sales department should have its own technical assistance helping out with customer presentations, but again, economy had to be considered, and not the least, could one find someone just as capable and suitable as an experienced developer for the job?

To avoid the "seed" to be eaten, one agreed to strengthen the technical support in the sales department, and inserted an ad.

No doubt it was a project taking time, but one was at least on the go.

The products were sold in many countries, and particularly in the flat neighbour country to the South, one had quite a sales activity, almost the size of the one in the mountainous North.

The overall long term company strategy was anyhow to look at the whole of Scandinavia as the home market, but that's another story.

The company in the flat neighbour country to the South also had their capacity problems but, as they didn't perform development, and was not meant to do so, the technical staff was closely connected to the sales and service department.

Also in that country they had many big projects going, and even if admittedly people from the mountainous country up North and the ones from the flat neighbour country to the South, to a certain extent could understand each other's language, there were certainly cultural discrepancies.

Customer relationship were not comparable on all levels, and in the flat neighbour country to the South, the products often needed special adaptation.

People there however, in many ways showed great creativity, and if they saw a chance to promote the systems in areas they were not yet prepared for, they didn't shy away going for it.

For that reason they one day got deeply involved in such a project with an existing customer, as it looked very exciting. Enthusiasm was common in both companies, both South and North.

The customer appointed a committee to form a trial project, and logically looked for cooperation with the company's technicians, something which of course was granted by the local forces. Everyone knew there was no development capacity in the mountainous neighbouring country up North to start such a project, but the customer pressed on.

Before anyone understood it, the customers hard working committee had already made a timetable for the entire project, which also directly influenced the working conditions for several employees.

During the assessment stage the technicians in the neighbouring flat land country to the South, kept continuous contact with the development department in the mountainous country.

Technical questions were asked and answered, and after a while one agreed that the development department should be engaged tree working days with some details related to tests required by the customer.

Soon it turned out that a few assumptions were not as clear as one thought, and the tree days became a week.

As most of us know it's not always easy to see the consequence of an act, so what happened was that even if the project was not registered as a task in the development department and thereby given a priority, one had to accept almost a 100% time violation.

When the test was made, it obviously led, as it always does, to continuous feedback, which again claimed non existing capacity from the development department.

The one led to the other, and before knowing it, all the consultations which mainly happened as innocent fragments on the phone, resulted in one month's engagement by the development department.

Discovering this, one made a deeper study and soon found out that the project which was initiated by the customer and which one at this time felt obliged to fulfil, was not even half way finished.

This way one had exceeded the original development time seven to eight times, and as mentioned already reached the point of no return.

All this had happened, as we understand, without the development department in the country op North really being engaged, and without there being any economical factor built in.

Suddenly one had created an insidious development in the neighbouring flat land country to the South, which officially was not planned.

This would obviously lead to repercussions demanding continuous support and follow up from the development department, again strongly charging their heavily loaded capacity.

The economy wasn't in the first instance the most important, but what do you think happened to those projects already prioritized and which already had a deadline?

14

Yes, this is what can happen in the fairy-tale world, as logically it can't be possible for things like this to happen in a well-organized company in the real world.

P.S.
No one must get the impression that this fairy-tale is a sad one. Of course, initiative is an important and valuable ingredient together with working effort, because without it all development will soon come to a standstill.

April 1999
GM.

Pointy nose - Jan Arnt 2010

Claim for Compensation

2016

Today is one of these days when one thing or another must be blamed on someone or even many.

Most of us probably have such days every now and then so surely, I'm not alone; but why then this heading?

The fact is that I never was too fond of neither Banks nor Insurance companies, something going back to the time I bought fifty percent of my stepfather's business, to become his partner in Max Manus Kontormaskiner (Office machines).

This happened in 1967 as a result of the company loosing it's two most important representations for office machines and communication systems, for non-self-inflicted reasons.

Not that it is of significant interest for this reflection, but the reason was that for example the office machine giant Olivetti, whom we represented in Norway as general agent, altered their company strategy to take care of the marketing on a word basis by themselves, while the other Swedish supplier of communication systems was bought by a larger concern.

Both these incidents made tremendous consequences for the continuation of the company, but that's another story.

My entry as a partner in the company implied of course also contact with the financial world and related obligations.

I hurry to make it clear that the daily economical part of business did not have my highest priority, although of course I fully appreciate that the purpose of business, first and foremost is to make money.

No special details or events led me to the above mentioned view on Banks and Insurance companies, they are a result from experience over longer periods, and have not become better after the latter years general development in the financial world.

I have been a pensioner for more than ten years, while my daughter and son in law owns and runs the business.

Particularly it is frightening to see how the Spanish banks seems to be permeated by corruption.

This country anyhow has big problems with corruption, but not making it an excuse, it must never be forgotten that it after all is not too many years ago, since a certain Franco had control of the society.

I am not competent to have meanings regarding this, but this event did, as most will understand, due to time delay Spain`s ability to create a culture most of us think is right. As we all know, things take time.

Without trying to understand details related to this I, despite my lousy Spanish, try to follow the daily news. I admit having problems with the understanding, but the main features I think I grasp.

Not one day without disclosures of one or another character. The last one, probably the most frightening for a long time, is the one related to Banco Madrid.

In Andorra, the Lilliputian society we all connect with a tax haven, Banco Andorra have stopped all payments. This to despair for all those believing that the bank was a safe nominee of their savings.

One man explained on the news that his savings of 850.000 Euro was about to disappear.

This of course is only bagatelles in the bigger picture, when one knows that tenfold if not hundreds of millions, by politicians are manipulated out of the country and placed there.

One country after another in South America have been involved in so called white washing through the same bank. Bankruptcies waving in the distance, with obvious consequences.

It is well known that the judiciary in Spain does not work very well, or at least not fast, so the implicit parties better plan for court cases lasting years.

"Where nothing is to be found even the Emperor has lost his right"

Not strange that the regular citizen loses confidence in the governing powers, which does not seem to be able to stop the development.

In Spain the law is apparently clear, bank deposits up to hundred thousand Euros are guaranteed by the state of Spain.

How that works in Andorra is unknown to me.

Every day the screen tells you, particularly the British one, that if you possess a bank deposit there, you are almost guaranteed to receive up to seven thousand Pounds in compensation, from so called "miss-sold payment-protection- insurance, or PPI".

Apparently, the banks have set off billions of Pounds to compensate for miss-sold insurances to customers.

Special vultures, in this case meaning dedicated law-firms guarantees the customers refund, costing them nothing.

Isn't it incredible what some "Good Samaritans" in the society does without charging for it.

Of course it is correct, the customer pays nothing directly, but who is paying for the expensive TV adds, and the fees and where does the money come from?

I am not in any way against the principal of so-called "No cure no pay", if only the deal explains the whole course. If that's the case I believe the principal has many good sides.

Apart from that it is incredible to get to know that banks having one year lost billions, the next year turns it around to a similar figure in plus. Have one ever heard of anything similar in ordinary business life?

Is anyone ever asking questions about how this is possible and what actions are needed to achieve such turn-around?

Most probably it's best not to understand it, as it could easily result in a to high blood pressure.

Concentration and Focus

March 2013

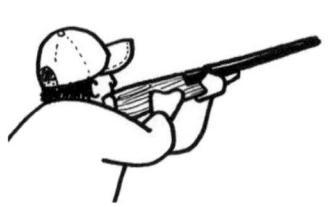

Concentration is an ability which I need to improve. How can someone be capable of claiming such a thing? How can someone say for sure that they have the capability to concentrate or, as in my case, that I need to improve my ability to concentrate.

How can it be measured?

Concentration means to be so involved in something that everything else disappears.

Now I have to concentrate on getting on with this reflection. I must in other words focus on the task, get so involved in it, that everything else disappears. How do I do that? Is it like looking down into a funnel where one at the bottom suddenly sees everything quite clearly, eureka?

Is there a connection between concentrating and focusing?

A lot of questions with the answers few and far between.

If there's something one can't do at any given time, it's easy to blame one's lack of concentration.

In the world of sports, the terms concentration and focus are well known.

Nobody wins if their concentration is absent and they lose the ability to focus on the task at hand.

This is especially obvious in the types of sports which stretch over time but where there is a constant need to perform to precision.

Golf comes to mind here as in many other contexts.

In a space of about four hours, which is what a round of golf usually takes, one has to perform as few strokes as possible, all of them can be different and there are up to 14 different clubs to choose between.

Around 70 strokes and below per round applies only to the very best players, while just over a hundred is the more normal number.

Each stroke requires full concentration and focus and the least disturbance, whether it be from the players themselves or in the form of unwanted thoughts and movements.

Any external influences can have dramatic consequences.

Regardless of the type of sport, it's often the ability to concentrate and focus which determines the winner.

Here is a typical example of my own lack of ability to ignore external disturbances in a sporting context.

Before I got into golf, I was for many years an active clay pigeon shooter, specifically in the area called skeet.

I'll never forget the episode in which I, during a championships competition over 100 clays, had fought my way through 99 hits and was ready for clay number 100. There was no lack of spectators but not a sound to be heard.

One more hit would lead to a new Norwegian record for 100 clays, so with my nerves totally on edge, I get ready for the last clay. Just as I call for the clay, which is thrown from a machine in a tower at an acoustic signal from my voice, I hear a voice say loud and clear: "Now he'll become Norwegian Champion".

The shot went off the moment I got a glimpse of the clay.

That was it. The amazing thing was that the person making the statement was the reigning champion.

The result was thus equal to the old record which for me, of course, was a big disappointment. It's quite possible that I would have missed anyway but, once again, at moments like this, the deciding factor is the ability to concentrate and focus.

Apart from a gold, silver and bronze medal in Norwegian Championship in team shooting, I personally never reached a top position in the individual Norwegian Championships. My best achievement was a bronze medal in August 84 in the open Norwegian Championship.

Up until the last 25 clays, I was often well placed for top positions. The skill was obviously there, but my lack of ability to concentrate, focus and control my competition nerves right to the end will have to take the blame.

My practise rounds were at times equal to the international top ones in those days. The best practice round ever was 197 out of 200.

For your information, in my days, normal skeet competitions lasted for two days, on which 100 clays were shot each day, so there were many waiting periods and distractions. Today the rules have changed.

It's far easier for me to concentrate when it comes to finding solutions to technical challenges.

Then it's easier to suppress other disturbing factors.

But then one is immersed in oneself, not exposed as during competitive sport.

It is said that one can train one's ability to concentrate.

This I don't doubt, I question, however, whether it's just as easy to get one's competition nerves under control.

That some people have better control over their nerves than others is quite clear and that there are those who have a far better ability to concentrate and focus than others, I also have no doubt.

Golden bird - Jan Arnt 2010

Confidence (The grumpy one)

2016

I start with an example which probably very few have got stuck by, but which made me lose confidence in the one in question, or rather, the institution representing her.

Well, this is probably not quite correct as, all considered, it has more to do with lack of awareness. I have touched this subject earlier in another reflection, as to the term: "In all Honesty". (Reflection II).

It's unbelievable that people can make such statements.

A well-reputed female reporter in CNN, which I will not name, came with the following statement recently: "I want to make a change in reporting by telling the truth". Have you ever heard something similar? Finally, we have one which contrary to other reporters has got it clear, she has decided to be honest.

Fortunately, the word advances.

Is there no control of what's happening, or rather what they broadcast?

Where is the censorship that otherwise take place anywhere else in our society?

What comes to mind as an example is the criticism of the slightest form of expression having to do with the strongly misused word racism.

In all fairness, it must be mentioned that the campaign was taken off the screen after a few months.

I hope that is a sign that someone after all is keeping an eye on things.

Another reporter I appreciate, as I also do in case of the above-mentioned, is the one which several times a day, slightly confused, is orientating himself through a labyrinth of green hedges before finally ending at a fountain. There he rings his famous bell making the water run, while full of enthusiasm expressing to us in front of the screen that he hopes we'll have a profitable day.

I don't mention his name either, but most probably you know who I mean.

Now way he himself being behind this stunt, and undoubtedly it can't be him deciding the frequency of the daily presentations.

What I find unbelievable is that they frequently present their reporters personally, with recordings having been on for many months. We know them all to boredom, the same way as "This is CNN – where the news comes first".

A good argument is of course that no one is forcing us to watch channels which are filled with self-glorification.

It's surely not the reporters themselves pushing this, although, for them it's obviously positive to get personal recognition by their employer.

Paid advertisements are probably the most important source of income in this context and that is of course OK. But could one not, as substitute for self-glorification, have a camera permanently mounted in a zoo and then maybe once a week make a snappy little gallery of the reporters?

Those of us being keen viewers anyhow have the pleasure of seeing them most of the time anyway.

The snag is to guess when the transmission contains news we haven't already seen.

I am not looking to hang out CNN in any way, as they are experts in drawing in elongation any so-called "Breaking news".

Probably, they aim to be the leader in this as well, as they already claim to be the world's largest and best news channel.

It's probably nothing they like to talk about, but I don't think I'm much off when claiming that CNN has a repetition-frequency of more than 65 %.

Reports are repeated infinitely, something they surely have sensible explanation for. One of them being that people only sporadically watching the channel, must also have a chance to catch up with old news.

That's only logical.

Apart from all this, it's not strange that it's easy to lose confidence in channels claiming they represent the correct truth, when one can clearly see that information's presented are tendentious and at times incorrect.

I have no problems with channels expressing political trends, those who don't hide their political point of view. That is OK with me.

Most people I believe, chose news channels according to their political views. One gets to know what one appreciate, and no one should be blamed for that.

To what degree one watch channels with divergent views to keep oneself updated, is of course one's own choice.

When trust strikes cracks, respect disappears.

Dizzy - Jan Arnt 2010

Consciousness – Unconsciousness

December 2014

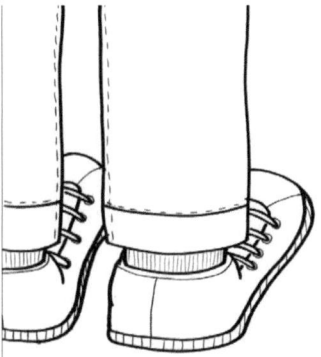

The shortest explanation I can get out of Wikipedia related to this contradiction goes as follows: "Only the ones with a functioning brain has consciousness, while unconsciousness is a common term for psychological processes a person is not aware of". To be conscious or unconscious is an either or. Either one is conscious or unconscious in a situation or action".

However, this cannot be resembled with Shakespeare's: "To be or not to be".

I can very well see that with this two extremes, either or, it becomes rather narrow. In between lies a sea of nuances.

Never the less, I in this case prefer to make it simple, conscious or unconscious. This way it's much easier to understand.

In this context it's not a matter of being unconscious in the sense of having lost the conscience when one is unconscious.

In that state of unconsciousness one is in no way capable of acting unconscious, one is fully conscious, but still unconscious.

Confusing of course, I can fully understand that.

Let me at once make clear that I surely at times, although I hope not too often, act as if I am unconscious, or, as I rather prefer to call it: being myself totally unconscious.

Normally I believe I am being conscious in the daily life.

My interpretation of that is that it amongst other must do with paying attention to the fact that one is not the only person on this earth, ore more realistic that one normally isn't the only person present where one is.

Not one day passes without me observing people acting unconsciously.

These days I travel less than before so most of my observations happens in our local area, mostly in the supermarket. There it happens all the time. People wander around the shelves in their own world, normally with their trolleys and often with a shopping list in their hand.

I don't dwell further with this, as all observant, conscious people will have registered to what an extent unconsciousness is wide spread in these surroundings.

The reason for this reflection to get to the paper has its background in an experience I had during our recent visit to Copenhagen.

December, board meeting, but also as usual a visit to the famous Tivoli. Fantastic Christmas atmosphere everywhere. In this context Copenhagen, can be recommended as a wonderful place to spend some days at this time of the year.

The traditional walk down Strøget, the famous pedestrian street stretching 1,1 kilometre is always an experience, particularly this time of the year when decorated for Christmas

We arrive from what I call the top, being the Town Hall and amble down Strøget.

As my wife and myself have been her almost every year since we married in 1998, we feel as at home.

A variety of entertainers make their most to make people stop, have a look and maybe leave some slings before they carry on.

Strøget, as the stretch is called start as mentioned at the Town Hall and it's first part is named Vesterbrogade. That turns into Nygade which then continues to Vimmelskaftet. After that one comes Amagertorget which brings you to Østergade. This one ends at Kongens Nytorv being only a stone through from the famous Nyhavn. With a row of characteristic small restaurants along the canal, the place is an experience.

Just having arrived at Østergade and without it being any tribulation I, suddenly feel an "axe hewed" to my right heel.

I scream out and sink into my knees.

Of course, it's not about an axe, but the hit was perfect to the Achilles scene.

When I get on to turn myself, I see two young men behind me, one with a trolley full of newspaper, more than a meter high, and the other with an umbrella and a little folder under his arm.

Both make excuses and behave exemplary, where after I found no reason to pull forward the deep voice.

26

I utter a comment that things seams to be all right and limp along, fully aware that what could have happened did not.

Earlier I have had a real accident with the Achilles scene so I know from experience what that means.

That story came as a result of my own fault and happened on the tennis court.

In his state of total unconsciousness, the master of the trolley was most probably engrossed in a discussion with his friend, the one with the umbrella and the folder.

Maybe you will give him a milder verdict than him being unconscious, for instance that he only was inattentive.

Black Bird - Jan Arnt 2010

Details

2017

In many ways it's a pity that details matter, as they are mostly boring and time-consuming to get in place. This I wrote about the details once in 2015.

Many details are boring but not all. For me it's like details often are boring, but if it's about a detail needed to be able to solve a challenge, I can be completely concerned about finding that detail, big or small.

Never the less, generally I am convinced that details matter, and that they often are boring.

In my book (Reflections I), I dealt with "The Bagatelle". That reflection was written in April 1994 and starts as follows: "I'm a tiny "bagatelle", a word, a smell, a taste. Spoken, felt or sensed, I can be a deciding factor in many contexts and of the greatest importance".

In the same way I believe it's often details that matter, and that is crucial.

It's often said that it's the small things that matter, here I am again, the bagatelle.

Doesn't it feel like the bagatelle is something small – a big bagatelle does not sound right, does it?

One of more descriptions of a bagatelle is: "A small and less important case".

A detail on the contrary, at least as I see it can, in addition to be small also be big.

Anyway, maybe the detail is most often seen in conjunction with something small: "The only thing missing is the little detail".

To me this is more a matter of platitudes.

One of more descriptions of a detail is:" Simplicity, part of a whole".

Well," simplicity" has nothing to do with size and neither has "a part of a whole".

After this it gets more dimension over the detail, doesn't it?

A detailed report is by no means a bagatelle, just as little as details in an account is.

Detailed descriptions of any kind one can only characterise as the opposite of having anything to do with the bagatelle.

If one look at examples like these, the "detail" and "the bagatelle" should not be used for each other.

Why on earth did I dig into these details when I can clearly see what dimensions they can occupy.

I was thought about the details in a non-academic way.

During my time schooling with Olivetti in North Italy as a 17-18-year old, I was trained to be a technical instructor. After my education, I was to teach our technicians, or mechanics as they were called in those days. During the end of the fifties all technical was still mechanical.

Not going to much into the details, but what is the difference between a technician and a mechanic?

According to Wikipedia: A technician is the professional title of a person with technical working tasks, while a mechanic is a craftsman using tools to repair machines.

As general agent for Olivetti office machines, our company Max Manus Kontormaskiner in Norway at the time employed about 40 mechanics, and had a dealer network with at least as many.

In those days, a spade was called a spade.

No form of discrimination, but today I have the impression that all in this group are engineers regardless of education, so in this context the details are probably not so important

When it came to repairing Olivetti Tetractys calculators with thousands of mechanical parts and more than hundred adjustments less than a millimetre, the details were of utmost importance.

Just one little adjustment wrong could be enough for the machine to fail after a reparation, so therefore that little detail could lead to the whole job to be done over again.

Before I wrote this reflection, I Googled "Olivetti calculators", hoping to find the exact amount of parts the Tetractys calculator consisted of, but didn't find it.

As mentioned many times in written, I am hopeless when it comes to data. I'm not part of any social media and as you understand barely capable to navigate on Google.

What strikes me however, is that when I hit "enter" after having Googled "Olivetti calculators", the first I see is the presentation of my last book: "70 years in communication" – about the Max Manus Companies from 1946 to 2016. (The Norwegian edition "70 år I kommunikasjon", as the English is not yet printed).

Of course, I understand that the Danish editor BoD (Bod.dk) are doing marketing, but that Googling "Olivetti calculators" should lead to my book is after my opinion quite clever.

I never got hold of the exact amount of parts in the Tetractys, but that detail, even if it is a matter of a few thousand, is presumably not important for those who have cared to read this reflection about the details.

Where are you going? - Jan Arnt 2010

Electronic Banking

September 2017

Of course, I have heard about «Electronic Banking», and of course I understand that one, by means of this tool, can perform money transactions.

That businesses are totally dependent of this method of working in relation to banks, and that this as well goes for the younger generation, and that it's a blessing for them, I'm in no doubt, particularly now as the bank branches don't exist any longer In Oslo.

Head offices yes, prestige is important and of course the administration must be housed, but what about the branch around the corner. Earlier it was there to facilitate the customer, a service obviously antiquated.

It must be due to the costs, as the fees of course are trifling as an income to keep them going.

The banks are the only institutions I know that one year can lose billions, and then the next year turn out even more billions in profit. How that is possible only the banks themselves knows.

We the customers know who is paying for it.

As I am resident in Spain, being thirty years behind in development thanks to amongst other a certain Franco, I am happy that they still keep the bank branch offices where all type of transactions can be made. Yes, they even deal with cash, would you believe.

Admittedly, you must be prepared for some latency, because as you will understand after having made a visit to one of them, the customer comes first. Half of the time spent with a customer, at least out of the big cities revolves around small talk. It's important that everyone is updated about the latest events.

I assume that "Electronic Banking" is widely used in Spain as well, something I, being close to eighty, is uninterested in. It has nothing to do with my lack of ability to take the challenge, but once saying yes, will of course lead to more.

I rather accept some latency in the local branch.

The last years we have normally spent the month of August in Norway to avoid the worst heat and tourist traffic, as we live in the most sunny part of Southern Spain.

During our visits we live in walking distance from the city centre of Oslo with its facilities. Apart from contact with my family and a few remaining old friends, we live a quiet life.

I skip a lot of details being part of this little story about "Electronic Banking", as it otherwise becomes too complicated.

About my book projects, I had my PC with me to Norway, I one of the first days received some invoices from the Danish Editor. Their maturity date was before we returned to Spain, and thus had to be paid from Oslo. They were in Danish kroner and was to be paid to the Editors account in the Danish Bank.

As I by chance discovered that the Danish Bank in Oslo had moved into new premises on Aker brygge, a commercial pier in Oslo, I paid them a visit.

In the big foyer with its large staircase leading up to first floor the receptionist, after I presented my mission, referred me to another more discreet entrance around the corner, after all I was only an ordinary customer.

With my British passport and my credit card from the Danish Bank, I introduced myself and explained my message to the lady attendant, and at the same time presenting my invoices which had to be paid.

Service minded and with a smile she shook her head and told there was no way they could help me with any transactions of that kind, that had to be done from a branch in Denmark.

That I had to pay these invoices before their maturity date to avoid severe consequences for myself, of course had no influence on her statement, nothing doing. I explained that I also had a credit card in the Norwegian Bank, but that it would be inconvenient to use it, as my account in the Danish Bank should be charged.

She suggested that the Norwegian Bank should pay them for me, and that I afterwards should tidy up my personal books. Furthermore, she added, the easiest way would be to use "Electronic Banking".

Well I answered, thanks a lot for your information, but please understand that I am not into the modern data technology and don't use "Electronic Banking". - Then I would advise you to start using it, she responded.

With a smile, I told her: «Being close to eighty, I suppose I belong to the last generation which don't live up to the modern times, and that's of course my own fault".

She seems to quite agree, as she gave me a "good luck" on my way out.

DNB – the Norwegian Bank's "Flaggskip" (Flagship), sounds very prestigious. They surely must be able to help a person in need?

I have passed the premises many times but have never entered the Bank before this day after my visit to the Danish Bank when I continued my stroll up to the Karl Johan street. (Main pedestrian street in Oslo)

I pull queue number 108 and register at the same time that number 93 is being processed.

The few seats for customers are occupied by a varied selection of Norwegians, and many are standing.

With a strange feeling that I, after a long waiting time, again could be short of a solution, I took "en spansk" something like a "Spanish action", (Not very flattering for the Spaniards, but a Norwegian expression of bending the rules).

One of the desks got a gap as the next number was a headed mother with four children, needing time to keep track on her ranks.

I took some resolute steps over to the desk, made an excuse and quickly presented my message. After having showed him both my Passport and my DNB card, he shook his head with a gentle smile and explained that this kind of transaction they could not perform. That's something you do by "Electronic Banking" he said. Oh - is that so, I exclaimed with a smile, at the same time asking if he knew of other solutions.

The headed mother was no approaching the desk with her two small ones in the pram pushed by the third, while the fourth had a solid grip on the mothers long black skirt.

Just as she presented her queue number 93, the sympathetic man behind the desk answered that the Post Office could also do this kind of transactions.

With a, many thanks for your help and a quick excuse to the black dressed mother and her kids, I again found myself on Karl Johan street.

Strange I've not thought about that before, it sounds totally logical that such a typical bank transaction is a job for the Post Office.

Well – that's when one understand how little one knows, but it's a good excuse that one has lived many years abroad.

Everything seemed now to be in order, and knowing where the Post Office was situated from before, and even having been there the same morning to buy stamps for my wife's postcards, it became my next goal.

A stroll in the light rain was quite refreshing, and as I on top only had to wait a few minutes with the queue number in my hand, I felt that Norway after all still represented the frontrunners regarding well organized Banking, providing of course you were familiar with the procedures.

The lady behind the counter was sympathetic and service minded. Again, the Passport, invoices and credit card in DNB were presented, and according to the lady this should be no match.

Out of a drawer she pulled a form where after she started filling it out.

As it was a matter of eight invoices she suggested they could be paid in one transfer to save transfer fees, which otherwise would be a considerable amount. That is what I call service I thought for myself.

Some ten minutes later, still filling out the form, she told me I would get a copy when everything was passed to the computer.

Imagine how easy things could be done without "Electronic banking", I thought, it's just a matter to know the procedure.

Suddenly she stopped keying.

All the time I had explained that the invoices were in Danish Crown's and she had even used a little calculator to cheque the rate of exchange and suggested I pay a little more to avoid later surprises caused by possible course deviation, something I of course accepted.

The reason she stooped keying was that she suddenly realized that payment was to be made to an account in the Danish Bank in Denmark. No, that could not be done, as the Post Office could only make domestic transfers.

All in vain. Here positive attitude came to a stop at the end of the run.

Thanking her for her efforts and making excuses for the inconvenience, I asked if she could give me any advices how to solve my challenge not using "Electronic Banking".

She knew that on the main Bus Terminal there were some offices doing transactions abroad, and that they possibly could help.

Again I thanked her and at the same time registered a row of people with queue numbers in their hands. They all threw less friendly eyes at me while making my way out.

The total operation had taken close to twenty minutes.

The alternative with the Bus Terminal, being situated on the other side of town, I found not to be an alternative, so I decided to make use of my "rescue plank", something I try to avoid not to disturb people in their work.

Easy for me being privileged, in the sense that I always have the possibility to use the family company in a pinch, but what about all those not having such possibility?

Does this mean that people my age, feeling that they have more meaningful things to do than to challenge new data technology, a race we anyhow will lose, are supposed to give up and lay in the oars?

Either way, why on earth should a pensioner my age put himself in a situation like the one described above?

Maybe I should stay home in Spain, where fortunately one can still pay one's invoices in the local Bank branch?

If I say yeas to "Electronic Banking", something I have no intention to do, most probably it would lead to other technical temptations I would have difficulty to resist.

Standing outside, not using "Electronic Banking", has its advantages. In this case for instance, I got the idea for this Reflection and a day with good exercise walking a few kilometres.

I quote a relevant Norwegian saying: "Even if bad, it's good for something." What about a new slogan:

"Against Electric Banking for elderly people – for exercise."

Punkbird

Sleepy bird - Jan Arnt 2010

Experience

Octobre 2013

There is something pretentious about the word experience: "Experience indicates…"As a general remark, in most cases one let it pass without closer reflection, but if presented in connection with serious posts, by people with authority, one better eject ears. Where would we be without the lessons experience teaches?

Wouldn't we just be repeating our actions, whether or not the repetition is justified. How often would we be correct in our repetition?

In our everyday lives we are not consciously aware of the way we use our experience. For the most of us we automatically draw our own conclusions. We base our experiences and subconsciously make minor or major adjustments.

As a result it is one of the main factors which help us develop throughout our entire life. It would be very sad if we at some point told ourselves that that's sufficient experience, let's flick the switch. In a way it would be the same as putting one's hands in the air saying that now I've got nothing more to learn, there's no point to the learning process. Those people who consciously acquire knowledge until the very end are the happiest.

It is of course true that theoretical knowledge also builds experience, though not immediately in a practical way.

Is there something called spiritual experience which complements practical experience?

Through school and universities one gets an academic education.

The experience one has gained as a result of one's studies are, of course, both valuable and necessary, one hopes, when it comes to applying for a job. But even when one's career choice isn't of a practical kind, but of a more academic type, the question of experience is always raised.

One stands there with one's exam results and is more or less treated the same as all the other applicants.

Regardless of who gets the position and the criteria used, one can ask oneself who should cover the cost in order to get the experience which has to be gained to do the job properly.

It's most likely the employer who has to invest in order to benefit fully from their employees' education, and that is probably as it should be.

Naturally enough one can't be equipped for the task one is given before one has gained the right experience.

A different situation involves education of a more basic character, which needs to be combined with business practice within a chosen profession. This combination of schooling and practical experience is in my opinion by far the best when it comes to career choices. I hope it still exists in some form or other.

At the time when I started working, at the end of the fifties, we had several apprentices employed in our firm. They were to reach their journeyman or trade examination. They were normally employed in the service department, had apprenticeship contracts and, if I remember correctly, were given one day a week off to attend the vocational school to get a theoretical education.

As far as I can understand, this arrangement has been replaced with other versions but I'm not up-to-date on this.

The question is if the apprenticeship scheme, in a more modernized form than the one we had back then, wouldn't be better and more interesting for many of those who feel the need to get into a craft early on, rather than fight their way through a higher theoretical education in which they have little or no interest.

I have heard that the apprenticeship scheme is practised successfully for instance in Switzerland and that in England there are constantly references to the fact that more apprenticeships ought to be created. I take this as a sign that this form of education is still considered the best when it comes to practical training.

I greatly believe in a working environment involving a combination of theoretical and practical training.

I have often heard it said "If only others could learn from our hard-earned experiences, how much better everything would be." That way of thinking is both short-sighted and meaningless in my opinion.

One has to be master of one's own experiences; I'll go so far as saying that it is only through one's own experiences that one can progress.

Here I exclude obviously well-accepted experience based on investigation and science. Such experiences belongs to all theoretical education on all levels and automatically provides a positive benefit in most cases.

In this context it is clear that knowledge can be drawn from other people's experience.

Not that one ought to believe that all experience is worthwhile, and I don't think anyone does. Everyone has, in one form or other, suffered bad experiences. The conclusion is that it isn't really important if one's experiences are good or bad as long as one learns from them.

Bad experiences don't trigger repeats, while the good ones ought to do so.

All of us should focus a little more on experiences, think through those of importance for one's personal development, and raise awareness of them.

I believe it would be good for us all to focus more on the value of experience. Think about the experiences one has benefited from in life, especially where one believes they have been important for one's development. Then become more conscious of them.

Most of us are, I believe equipped with a good - or not so good - ability to suppress bad experiences. I call this ability a safety valve.

We can't keep filling up with too much negativity, especially as regards the bad experiences we suffer from at times.

We ought to suppress some memories of them, when we feel that it is necessary, in order to maintain an acceptable balance.

The best experience which have contributed to my development, I believe I gained during my time at school in Italy from nineteen fifty-seven to fifty- eight.

Fanaticism

May 2014

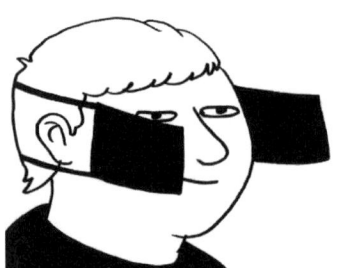

Even though it's probably clear to most of us what fanaticism means, I'll start, just in case, with a description from Wikipedia which says that fanaticism is: "Extreme one-track mindedness. Passionate claiming of personal convictions, often combined with wanting to persecute those who think or feel differently".

It almost makes me shudder when the word fanaticism is read or heard, or even just by thinking about it. Only in very special cases can I, at least, find something positive in connection with fanaticism, and then it has to do with personal fanaticism, for instance when one is fanatically concerned about something special. That kind of fanaticism is probably in most cases completely harmless.

Its limits are clear for most of us, but not for everyone, and that is probably what makes fanaticism so dangerous.

What I find somewhat strange is that an English description of fanaticism is more or less in line with the above, in other words with the personal and harmless one. It goes more or less like this: "Fanaticism is a belief or attitude involving uncritical eagerness or exaggerated enthusiasm as regards past-time activities or hobbies". Well, if that had been the only angle of fanaticism, lots of things would be different.

Many have tried throughout time to analyse the fanatic, he or she who represents fanaticism. When that happens it has mainly to do with that which most of us consider dangerous fanaticism.

The general consensus seems to be that fanatics as such aren't evil in the strict sense of the word, they, the fanatics, are just fanatically convinced that the opinions they represent are the only correct ones. There is never any talk of compromise, seen from a fanatic's point of view, so the idea of using diplomacy where the fanatic is concerned, can immediately be shelved. The greatest danger lies in the fanatic's ability to influence the weak or misguided, examples of which we see every day.

Well, I am, of course, not competent to add anything at all as regards fanaticism, but, on the other hand, I am concerned about one's and for all having to put an end to this evil, the dangerous one, that is. One has to be realistic though, to believe that one can get rid of the dangerous fanaticism, is to aim too high.

If one wants to try to do that, one has to apply other measures, at least if one has a long-term solution in mind. Just imagine finding a sensible answer to that challenge.

In many areas it is totally acceptable to refer to statistics.

Of course, one can't always trust the statistics, but that has nothing to do with those involved not being able to gather the right material, but with the fact that the material has been manipulated in order for the statistic to show the desired result.

Regardless, there must be a statistic showing the percentage of population who are fanatical according to the definition. I don't doubt that at all, but I believe one is reluctant to make it official. Some probably feel it could lead to social consequences.

Is the percentage of people who are fanatical according to the definition, the dangerous one if it can be isolated, greater or smaller than five percent, or is it more than ten percent?

Is the percentage of population who are fanatical according to the definition, the one described in the English interpretation, greater or smaller than five percent, or is it more than ten percent?

Would our knowing the size of the percentage have any significance at all for the rest of us in our daily lives?

Personally I am of the opinion that there are far more fanatics amongst us than we believe, in fact, I'd go as far as putting myself down as a potential candidate, as regards the English interpretation, the one I believe to be harmless.

How can I say that? Well, there are things in our every day lives that I can be fanatically concerned about, without my wanting to disclose what they are.

This because it has nothing to do with a permanent condition and because I know that this form for fanaticism is a completely harmless one, at least for others. Whether it might be dangerous for me is another matter.

What I'm trying to say, in other words, is that fanaticism as such isn't necessarily dangerous. It's only if it's used incorrectly, according to most of us, that it becomes dangerous.

The dangerous fanatic is usually someone who chooses his followers with great care. Trust is created and solid friendships are made. The followers are usually simple and easily influenced people, and thus fit easily into the role of performing the evil transmitted through the relationship. In this role the fanatic is mortally dangerous.

If we stay with this latter description, of the dangerous fanatic, I trust that an honest statistic would verify that only a fraction of one percent of the population belongs to this category, at least in our part of the world, which is a good thing, if my assumption is correct.

Even if there is little each and everyone of us can do to expose these potential "bomb threateners", it is important that we make our beliefs and attitudes clear, so that we and those of like minds won't be subjected to unexpected ambushes.

Siamese twins - Jan Arnt 2010

Feeling of Guilt

April 2013

Feeling of guilt; it makes me shudder just thinking of it. Not that I believe I have reason to feel guilty, but there's no doubt that I'm one of those people who gives off an aura of guilt. This being the case even though I, at least in my own opinion, have no reason to do so.

Perhaps it has something to do with my adolescence.

I definitely used to toe the line in my youth. There were seldom serious wrongdoings but there was something about having to try things out. It's important to find out where to draw the line as the parents don't always offer appropriate guidelines.

If one is born with imagination and empathy, consequences are bound to follow.

My stepfather had a clear idea of where the line had to be drawn, everything he saw as serious wrongdoings was measured in a certain number of strokes from the dog whip, it was as simple as that.

In many situations this is probably a good method of settling things but according to today's standards apparently far from the right one. We mustn't forget that this was more than sixty years ago and a lot was different in those days.

Enough said, I believe that I at that time found the punishment just. If I had toed the line, that it was the price one had to pay. Otherwise the only alternative one could see to avoid the punishment was to run away from home. I don't believe that would have solved anything. I also don't believe my mother was quite in tune with the punishments but having a domineering husband, she chose to keep peace on the home front. At least I never registered any arguments between them on this subject. The threat of being sent to the correctional institution on Bastøy in the Oslo fjord also remained in the background, but was from my side probably never seen as a real possibility.

That was in my opinion like shooting sparrows with a cannon, nor did it ever happen.

A feeling of guilt we probably all experience in some form or other. One only has to look around among one's own family and friends. Whether the feeling of guilt is justified, only the person involved can say.

When I mentioned earlier on that feelings of guilt may have to do with one's adolescence, I was perhaps quite wrong. My younger half-sister, who never did anything wrong when she was little, has undoubtedly all her adult life had problems with her feelings of guilt. Could it have something to do with one's nature and not with one's nurture?

In my case, the conscious feeling of guilt first occurred at school. There's no reason to hide that I was a so-called troublemaker in class, but it was as far as I remember never suggested that whatever I did had a nasty intent.

It's strange to see, but my youngest grandchild, who is fifteen this year, has apparently had the same sort of struggle at school for the last few years. I have been given to understand that he undoubtedly also is a mischief-maker in class.

I have no difficulty facing reality today, and I see that many of the reprimands were justified.

But what about the other side of the coin? Often as a result of the above, one automatically got accused of things one hadn't done or taken part in? That was sometimes hard to swallow as one felt that one had got enough from the obvious wrongdoings. It was thus registered as deeply unfair and difficult to understand.

So I ask myself the question: Is there a clear link between injustice and feelings of guilt? I can't quite come to grips with it, but I have a feeling I'm on to something essential here.

This probably won't stop me using injustice as a separate theme for a reflection. It is after all a huge subject to write about when one thinks about all the injustice there is in the world.

Regardless, my feeling of guilt has fortunately decreased over the years.

At one time, I could never go through passport control without being called aside for a closer check.

The customs officers had a special eye for me, almost as if I were some sort of regular problem to them. I can't remember ever having been caught carrying anything I shouldn't or my "quota" being exceeded. I don't want anyone to consider me sanctimonious in this context, but just because I believe my bad conscience could be sensed from afar, it was a contributing factor to my never carrying anything more than that which was within the allowable limits. This applies to the present as well as the past.

I mentioned the possible link between injustice and feelings of guilt, but now conscience comes into play.

I've already written a reflection about conscience. In it there is something about suppressing one's feelings of a bad conscience and the warm glow one gets from a good one. Conscience probably belongs in this reflection too because I don't suppose there's anything called good or bad feelings of guilt, is there?

After this, the question will have to be changed to: Is there a link between injustice, conscience and feelings of guilt?

It is time to get off this track before I start spinning out of control, as so far it has become complicated enough.

As some of you will have noticed, it has so far, apart from my half-sister, only been about my own relation to feelings of guilt. The reason for this must be that it is virtually impossible to describe other people's feeling of guilt as that's a very private matter

Full House

2015 – 2017

The heading does not directly reflect the content of this little story.

Triana is our favourite restaurant, and as one will understand, not only because it's situated in our Urbanisation and for that reason is very convenient.

The owner is Guillermo and his mother Mari Carmen is the Chef. We have had the pleasure of following the development from it's opening, as we already from that period were established in the Urbanisation Valle del Este in the South of Spain. It is situated not far from the towns Vera and Garrucha, in the Almeria region of Andalucia.

Mari Carmen is from Valencia, while Guillermos's father is from Aljeciras close to Gibraltar.

It all started with Guillermo working as a servant in the newly opened hotel in Valle del Este.

He was from day one liked by everyone and popular.

The Commercial Centre, being built at the same time as the hotel, is situated just a stone throw from the eastern part of the hotel, and it didn't last long before Triana, or Hojo 19 (Hole 19) as the restaurant is now named, opened. This happened in 2008. The family put all their efforts into the running of the place, which would turn out to be a success.

Mari Carmen had, many years before they started in Valle del Este, managed a popular restaurant in Soto Grande, near Gibraltar.

Guillermos father, Felix, was also part of the set up, but played a passive role.

As Triana's popularity increased, followed the demand for expansion and in 2010 around 100 guests could be attended simultaneously.

Under the management of Mari Carmen, two Romanian assistants, Elena and Carmen, were trained in her diversified cocking skills and are today fully qualified in preparation of the culinary.

Guillermo, which personally takes hand of his guests, have proven to be a qualified HR manager and throughout the years we have only had superlatives regarding the rest of the staff.

At present the core of the permanent staff dealing with the clients are Juanjo, Brook an Grego.

Brook is the youngest and last employed, English, but raised in Spain. She lives in the Urbanisation.

They are all friendly and have an eye on each finger. Juanjo, living in the Village of Gallardos about five kilometres away, has a positive infecting attitude. Grego, living in the nearby city of Vera is, without discrimination of the others, very special in a positive way.

We got to know her long before she came to Triana, while she was working in another restaurant. Already then, we registered her special personality and positive attitude.

She has now worked for Guillermo a few years and for us she stands out as an example of how a waiter should deal with the tasks at hand. She has worked in the trade for many years, and have brought numerous clients from her earlier working places.

Throughout the winter season we have lunch at least once a week at our reserved table, while in the summer half year we prefer visits in the evenings.

The food and the atmosphere is top, and it's visible that the place is popular amongst the Spaniards, as they represent most the guests, apart from the golfers which after their round like to meet on the terrace for the traditional drink after their challenge.

Having read the above, the reader may have expected something about Triane being filled up by customers, hens the heading "Full House".

Even if that happens during special events, as an example on Fridays in the winter when they arrange Flamenco dancing or other form of music events, that isn't the "Full House" concerning this Reflection.

We seldom drink coffee at home, mostly tee, but when eating out we both normally take a cup instead of having desert. This however normally only after lunches, seldom dinners.

Should the latter happen we will always ask for them to be decaffeinated.

In Triana we have the arrangement that if we don't let them know that we don't want coffee, it is automatically served.

My wife get an "Americano con Hielo" (American with ice), while I get my "caffe con leche" (Coffee with milk).

For my wife the ice is served separate in a glass and she will herself poor the coffee from the cup to the glass. Mine is a matter or ordinary coffee with milk.

What you have read so far was put on paper in July 2015.

Since then they have made big changes.

The restaurant has gone through a total rebuilding and today present itself with a totally new face.

Both Brook and Grego have for various reasons left, and as this little story saw daylight resulting from an input from Grego, I have made slight changes to the manus.

One day when Grego served us the obligatory coffee after a better lunch, I came to ask her how many different recipes of coffee she could serve.

With a smile she told that she once had served a table of sixteen Spaniards. This happened before she started working in Triana. When they reached to the coffee, all sixteen had ordered their own version. In other words, their own special variety, or recipes, from her portfolio.

For me, with limited knowledge about coffee, that seemed something of a joke, so I asked her if she put the various recipes down on a piece of paper. I had already in mind to put something on paper about Triana, and told her so.

No problems for Grego, as she said she had many more than sixteen up her sleeve.

Next time we came for lunch she handed me a list with the sixteen recipes she had served, without further comments.

For various reasons this reflection was not given any priority before now in 2017.

When I came to think about the sixteen coffee-servings, it came to me that this reflection about Triana should have the new heading "Full House".

But then the challenge, what had happened to the list from Grego?
　　Wherever I looked I couldn't find it.
　　Well, my original plan I suppose, was never to make a detailed list of the various coffee recipes for the readers to go through.
　　Probably a search on Google would satisfy any coffee lover.

I leave it like this and choose to believe there are few which can copy Grego in serving a "Full House" of different Coffee recipes to a table of sixteen.

The tree number men - Jan Arnt 2010

In the middle of my professionally active life

1989

One makes many reflections when one find one-self in the middle of ones professional active life. One logical question would be: When in time do I find myself in the middle of it, assuming of course that I live a normal long life? Next year I turn fifty, and have been active in the business world proxi-mately 30 years.

Under normal circumstances this would represent about 2/3 of a profes-sional active life.

How can I then regard it as half gone?

Although I don't run as fast as I did 20 to 30 years back in time, I claim that the experience gained through these years, fully compensates for all the running and thereby makes me more efficient.

What is efficiency?

I have easily convinced myself that today I make decisions, in this case the real unpleasant and challenging ones, in a fraction of the time I needed for the same 20 to 30 years ago, and I urge myself to say, with equally good if not better results.

Despite always having been a "talker", I feel the improvements also have been gained in that respect.

Meetings are deliberately forced to be more rational end effective.

Could the reason be that one takes on more and more challenges and thereby become more time conscious and more precise to be able to imple-ment these challenges?

As the overall dream is to slow down a notch as one takes on years, this don't not match with still taking new challenges. But then again, if one doesn't do it, take new challenges that is, one has not become more effec-tive.

Quite a different subject is that I have also studied if one has become more effective by sifting out unwanted information's.

Being totally honest to oneself, something one of course is, it happens one has a feeling that's being the case.

Surely, it's not easy. Seen from one angle, one want to paint a good picture of oneself, to oneself, at the same time as one must admit that it becomes more difficult to honestly say that one is in the middle of one's professional active life around 50 - maybe 2/3 after all is more correct?

Personally I have for a long time used the thesis that: "Everyone is right from their prerequisites".

Isn't that why politicians are quarrelling – marriages are dissolved and wars take place?

Imagine if more of us had the ability to see things objectively – think how much easier it would be to solve common challenges.

How much time is spent in vain in discussions, only for someone to feel they are right?

Obviously, I can see things objectively. Imagine how good it is to be able to say that, it really makes me feel I am right.

Do I waste less time – do I have a foot in each camp – am I still married to the one I promised to share live with to the end.

Have I not created enough "mini-wars"?

It's a good feeling to be in the middle of one's professional active life, whether it's 2/3 or half way through.

Imagination and Product Development

March 2013

"Imagination is the ability to picture something, especially that which doesn't exist in reality. The ability is used to create art, but also to find solutions to problems". This is what Wikipedia says in its simplest explanation. For my part, I would prefer to replace "problems" with "challenges", it sounds much more positive.

Faced with challenges, one's imagination is triggered, whereas a confrontation with problems might seem less inspiring to deal with, at least that's the way it is for me. It can't be more clearly put: Without imagination, there's no innovation, imagination is the driving force.

That doesn't mean, however, that one automatically can become a great artist or inventor just because one's imagination is good, far more is required. Curiosity is in my opinion, as mentioned in a separate reflection about this ability, also a requirement, along with a will to solve challenges and a large amount of work effort.

I feel that curiosity often comes first, as when one is curious one's imagination gets going. Anyway, seeing this put to paper, it might also be the other way around, so that if one has imagination, one's curiosity is triggered.

When imagination is coupled with innovation and product development, one probably needs a basic idea to start with, one can't just pull an unknown out of one's pocket, or is that just the way it works? Spontaneity is probably also a necessary ingredient in one's ability to create, isn't it?

Suddenly and without warning one gets an idea, which leads to other things.

But don't think an idea is worth anything on its own.

It's what you do with the idea which counts.

Far too many times in my life I have met people who have had the world's most ingenious ideas. The human being is just grand, the idea doesn't exist which hasn't entered someone's mind, probably far more than one thinks, naturally enough without their having been given credit for it.

That's because others with similar ideas have managed to do something about them, converted them to reality in the form of practical results. One often meets people who when they are confronted with an idea, answer: "I've often thought about that". Worthless, we are here back to the hanger-on or follower, he or she who often says: "that's what I've always said" or "that's what I've always thought or felt". The fact is that they for various reasons haven't had the ability to do something with the idea. It, the idea, remained just that, an idea, and as such also remained worthless.

Imagination and interest also belong together. Interest is a very broad term. If one is talking about development in the sense of product development, which I in this case prefer, interest probably comes first, if one hasn't got "this special idea", seemingly out of nowhere. There are those who claim that: "I've been pregnant with this idea a long time now". The question is if one's subconscious doesn't play a part in this in a lot of cases. If one is working with a challenge on one's mind over a period of time, the solution often appears as if served on a plate, one's subconscious works on the quiet.

First the area of interest to be focused on has to be identified. Having done so and then letting one's imagination loose, one has got a process going.

One's imagination has no limits it is said and that is probably true, but in this process, in terms of product development, that is, it is important to be able to control one's imagination. If it's let loose uncontrolled, it might all become unrealistic.

One mustn't tighten the reins too much, of course, as then one might restrict the result. This delicate balance is incredibly important.

In other words, one has to learn to balance imagination and realism.

In other contexts, when it has nothing to do with development, it is great to let one's imagination run free, after all, it has no limits, and that's what imagination is all about.

Some have an easier time using their imagination than others.

Back to product development. Good ideas rarely fall from the sky. One must from the start have an interest in one's chosen area as well as a positive attitude; don't forget: "Nothing enters into a closed hand".

One can't let one's imagination loose if one has already put the brakes on, either by not having a positive attitude or by focusing on problems to be solved instead of challenges which can be met.

Inspiration also forms part of that which is needed, I believe. I wrote a reflection about inspiration in 1994 wherein I asked, among other things, the question about where inspiration comes from and if it is synonymous with creativity.

At that time I kept to the subject of music and pictorial art, so it's fitting that I should think about imagination largely in connection with development at this point, especially when one hears that the word means: empathy, inhaling, perception, enthusiasm and divine impulse.

Perhaps imagination is, when all is said and done, like the icing on the cake.

Without any order of precedence, it becomes clear to me that imagination exists in almost all contexts.

I see imagination as being tied to and playing an important part in: inspiration, curiosity, interest, positive attitude, overcoming challenges, work effort, spontaneity and ideas.

Seafood - Jan Arnt 2012

Inauguration

1997

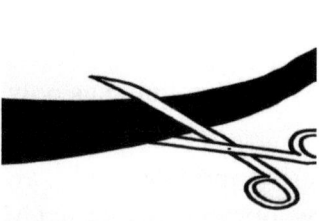 Only a few hundred meters from the last building in a row of many, in the outskirts of the village, a red silk ribbon is crossing the road. The ribbon is on each side linked to shiny brass poles, each fixed to solid iron plates not to make them tilt. They usually have their place in the "Salon de Plenos" in the town hall.

The Mayor of the village, a bachelor with a big black moustache, the priest and the president of the Deputacion Provincial De Almeria, the nearest city of any size and his party, are the font figures in the event which is going to take place.

The time is about ten in the morning, and the members of the music band in their colourful uniforms are standing in a group talking, awaiting further instructions.

A few hundred of the village inhabitants have found their way to the sight, as information about the happening had been spread. Even in the year ninety eight, information's about events taking place, as for example this, are broadcasted to the inhabitants of the village through an amplifier system with strategically placed loudspeakers all around in streets and markets. Maybe an effective insurance that information's also reach those whom never read newspaper, nor listens to the local radio. Although you will find bars on almost every street corner, maybe the most effective way to spread information is via these public address systems.

The event, which is going to take place, is the inauguration of the six kilometres long stretch of road which from now on will be the main entrance to the urbanisation called Cabrera.

The road itself have existed as long as anyone can remember and even long before that, but only in the form of a dusty approach to the big old finca, whereof the ruins still remains in the middle of the urbanisation. The road is making its way further up the mountainside and reaches more than seven hundred meters above sea level before it again turns down on the other side. From the place where the road turns the highest point, there is a magnificent view along the chain of mountains both towards the east and west, while at the same time one can see the curving of the Mediterranean See, which nearest shores are less than ten kilometres away. The highest peak will be to the right of the road after its turn on the top, and reaches just thousand meters.

Until today this road, even the stretch up to the urbanisation, has only been safely passed by using four wheels drives.

The road which has been used until now to bring residents and visitors up to the place, was constructed when the development was started in ninety eighty tree, and was paved at the same time. It enters the urbanisation from the opposite side, is much steeper and a little bit longer from the main road.

The Guardia Civil is represented with a newly washed characteristic green and white lacquered car and four uniformed officers. The Policia Local with their blue and white Nissan four wheel drive presents two policemen.

In less than a week, a very efficient gang of workers with all modern equipment, have prepared and made the road ready, before it, only days ago was covered with tarmac. From a birds view one can now see the big black snake which is curving through the undulated landscape up to the urbanisation.

If this event had happened only half a year earlier, she would have arrived in her, at the time, thirteen years old white Ford Fiesta, but now she is turning out from the village in a snappy little red sporty Korean.

She has scarcely parked, before the Mayor opens the car door, helps her out, and gives her the classical kisses on both chins. All the time since her, quite older than herself husband passed away about four years earlier, he has had a good eye at her, but in all fairness it has to be said, she has never given any encouraging response. Once, she recalls, it never the less came so far that she had to tell him that she had a son his age. After this event, and after it was well known to everyone that she had started a new relation, a more professional and business like contact emerged with him. He had at this point in time only been the Mayor of the village a little more than a year, but the mill of bureaucracy down there in Southern Spain was still not turning very fast. That is why, if you are in business, a frequent contact with the authority is necessary to keep the wheels turning.

With her experience from more than twenty five years in Spain, she has a deliberate non existing relation to local politics, and therefore she is riding on a wave of personal contacts built up over the years, which do not involve political prestige from the ones she is professionally involved with in business. During the time she has lived in the area, the village has had tree Mayors, one representing the conservative party, one the socialists and one the independents.

As time passes by, more people are finding their way to join the event, and even if we are in the latter part of March, the heat reaches close to thirty centigrade Celsius.

The band finally gets their starting signal. Whirls from the drums are the initiation of a couple of well-known marches, which are followed by the unavoidable speeches. They, at occasions like this obviously belong to the seen. When the priest as the last speaker is giving the road its blessing with a pointed finger in the air, he reminds the public that the blessing is only valid for those who respect the speed limits of the thirty and forty kilometres per hour. The crowd burst out in laughter, and the time has come for the big moment.

Where she stands together with the Mayor with the pair of scissors in her hand, ready to cut the ribbon, it strike her that she in a way has come to a turning point in her life. As by a strike of lightening, thoughts brings her back to the first time she left her home country Switzerland and started working in Ibiza, and the life which she has been through until she now stands her ready to cut the ribbon which officially opens the new entry road to the urbanisation which, both for her and her late husband, has given so much pleasure, but also has cost so much blood, sweat and tears.

In the total lack of movement in the air, the ribbon which is now cut in two, falls down towards the black tarmac, and is pulled towards each brass pole. This way an opening is made, through which the row of cars can start their slow drive up to Cabrera.

For her this represents a symbolic start of a new phase in her life.

Jealousy

January 2012

It's now about fifteen years since my last reflection was put to paper.

At the time I had a whole page full of titles for future reflections and still do, but since then a lot of changes have taken place in my life. Most of them, when it comes down to it, have only been to the good, but as a result none of the titles have been turned into reflections.

Nor did they die, but other challenges took the driver's seat, so the urge to continue had to make way for other activities.

All the reflections which saw the light of day at that time, were dictated more or less uninterruptedly into my Pocket Memo, a little Philips cassette player, and subsequently played back and listen to while two fingers on the keyboard turned them into written words, first on the screen then onto paper.

This is the first time the same two fingers have put reflections on the screen directly from the keyboard without the aid of a tape.

Today it would be quite natural to update the same cassette player by replacing it with an electronic device on which the voice is transferred to a fixed storage element. Anyway, the result would not have affected the content.

The big question is, as more than fifteen years have gone by since the last reflection, will the style stay the same and the form be maintained, or will everything be different?

Will the priorities and the content be led by inspiration? Have the events and personal experiences of the last fifteen years brought on changes, as a result of one's having sailed the seas longer and thus having more ballast in the tanks?

These will remain just thoughts for the time being.

Perhaps this will be my only attempt.

At least it has ended up with my grabbing hold of Jealousy, one of the titles on my list of future reflections.

It doesn't have anything to do with the alphabetical order of the titles; however, it just seemed to be the most obvious choice, like it was important to get it over and done with.

Jealousy, this terrible disease, which isn't normally terminal, but which slowly but surely leads to destruction, whether it be of friendship or any other kind of relationship.

Nor does jealousy have to do with gender, anyone can catch the disease.

Let me at once get out of the way the one which has to do with someone being jealous of things belonging to others. It can be difficult enough to deal with and even dangerous in a greater context. For instance for countries who are rich in oil and gas, large fresh water reserves or other valuable raw materials or natural resources which others don't have.

I choose to stick with the jealousy most of us are familiar with in one way or other, the one which with certainty leads to destruction.

The question is if it's hereditary or if it happens as a result of circumstances, situations one has lived through or other external influences. Regardless of which, it's terrible.

My experience is that those who are prone to this form of jealousy seem to nurse it along by watering and fertilizing it like the keenest gardener, and grow it does.

I've often wondered if those in question are aware of their disease. I don't believe they are, because if they were, as otherwise sensible people, they should be able to find an antidote; that, however, I've never seen an example of. There doesn't seem to be a cure.

Jealousy always affects someone, regardless of the form it takes. Someone is always made to suffer. When the jealousy is justified, I look quite differently on the disease; in fact, I might even be willing to retract it from the diseases.

I see it as a justified reaction, an expression of possibly righting a wrong. That's not the jealousy I'm concerned with, however.

That's not the type of jealousy which festers, because here there is normally a party who deep down feels that the criticism received is justified, if he or she has some sense of reality.

This type of jealousy I understand and can live with should it apply to myself.

No, we're back to the form of jealousy which is unjustified, that's the worst disease. It's one-way, arguments and realities have no place here, and it's totally irrational.

Even the most tolerant being has no defence against it, seldom can one say that "to give up" is the right thing to do, but in this situation it is, in my opinion, the only resort.

This must be one of the few cases where I find that to throw in the towel is correct. I actually think that this disease, this unjustified form of jealousy, viewed from the described angle, is totally destructive and without hope.

This reflection is probably subjective, seen through the eyes of most people and it only seems right to admit that my own personal experiences have influenced its content.

Anyway, if you are one of the lucky ones who hasn't become acquainted with jealousy from the described angle, you should be happy about it.

If you feel that you're on the same wavelength, however, it can only make you feel good to know that you're not on your own in any way.

Duel - Jan Arnt 2010

Kidnapping in Sweden

April 2014

This could very well be the title of a thriller by Stig Larsson, but far from any resemblance apart from that. In this case it is all about a short but true story, which for all those not involved obviously is an insignificant experience only representing a couple of pages on paper.

This happened almost seventy years back in time, in 1945.

Even if I in a way was the main character in the incident, this is of little importance. I could just as well have been a modest lump of gold, or a document, valuable only to the ones involved.

Mother married in 1936 my British father George Bernardes. They lived in England, and only months after I was born in 1939, she left the marriage for Norway and took me with here.

My father, after the Germans invaded Norway in 1940, was stationed as the British consul in Haugesund on the South-East Part of the country, with the main task to oversee the German shipping traffic.

As the Germans got foothold in the country he ended up in Åndalsnes, quite further up the coast. As he stayed there the town was totally levelled by German bombing, and the house where he was living got a full hit. He was hit in the head by several metal splinters, but survived against all odds, though with lasting after injuries for the rest of his life.

The Germans, after he was released from the hospital in Ålesund, took him to Vollan prison in Trondheim. Thereafter to another German prison in Oslo called Møllergata 19, and then, thanks to his diplomatic status, he was exchanged to Sweden.

After having gone through tree operations by the famous brain surgeon Olivecrona, he ended up as a convalescent at Saltsjøbaden, where-after he got status as Vice Consul in Stockholm.

My later stepfather Max Manus and mother had met many times in Stockholm while my mother worked at the British Legation, and had decided to merge if they survived the war. Max was during the war a very active saboteur in Norway.

Nothing more to dwell over, when a relationship is over, it's over - life goes on.

What follows is directly copied from my mother biography, Tikken Manus – the saboteur's secret teammate, penned by Kaja Frøysa in 2008. I have permission from NRK Atrium to print the following cut from the book.

"Tikken had no misgivings as for the plan she had.

By travelling to Norway for good together with little George, she wanted to prevent the father to make contact with the son.

Tikken burnt all papers, got rid of the poison pills not any longer needed and closed the office in Stockholm.

Friday the same week she called the summer camp and instructs the manager within to prepare the boy for being picked up next morning. The manager within knows only that the boy is picked up a few days before the deal, consequently no questions asked.

It became an unbearable tense Saturday morning, was I to get away without being discovered.

George Bernardes had Diplomatic Status and Tikken feared he would call the border police which again could stop her from taking the boy out of the country.

In the morning George leaves as usual for the Consulat and Tikken is alone for a few hours.

She gathers some clothes in a suitcase.

Andreas Aubert was one of our friends in Company Linge. He was going to help me into Norway.

Andreas came to collect me this morning, with a car. We drove to the summer-camp where little George was ready to travel. In half an hour we took to the road again towards the Norwegian border. Andreas Aubert drives as fast as possible on the curvy road and in the back scat Tikken clans up what she can of what the son has thrown up. There is no time to stop.

I was convinced that if stopped I had to give up little George. In such case I had gone after him, something else I had not been capable of. If we only made it over the border, I would get all juridical help from my father and brother.

Later, George Bernardes denies that he tried to prevent Tikken from travelling home to Norway, but for her the fright was there and very realistic.

Little George didn't understand why mamma and the chauffeur was so nervous, but the fear infected him.

Even if the kidnapping happened more than sixty years ago, he still has strong memories about it."

"I thought I was going to die during the trip, not because of the war or that my father should stop us, but due to my miserable condition. I didn't understand the seriousness of the situation, but my mother and Andreas Aubert were very nervous.

Aubert did chose to cross the border at Ørje, and that seemed to be a good choice . They were not stopped, neither by the border police or the customs officials.

It went better than we could have hoped for. I will never forget when we had passed the border. We sat down close to a little lake. It was a beautiful day that day the 12th of June 1945. I told George that we should soon meet aunt Kari and Grandpa again. Andreas and myself had a little drink to celebrate before proceeding to Oslo Grand Hotel, where Max received us.

It was unbelievable to see him again, and to be on Norwegian soil with him. Now we could take a breath"

In my personal presentation speech in my Rotary Club I 1987, about twenty years before my mother's memoirs were written, I mentioned this episode in my life. (The whole speech is included in my book Reflections II).

I include the part directly related to the "kidnapping".

"The summer of 1945, was perhaps the start of that part of my life which was seriously concerned with my development and awareness of environmental influence.

The middle of the day, lovely sunshine, I recall. The place being a summer camp way out in the Swedish country-side. A car arrives with my mother and an unknown man inside. My belongings were packed and off we went. I became carsick at the time and have been frequently so ever since.

There was apparently a lot of excitement at the Norwegian border; I had some odd thoughts, but was to young to understand. Had my father, who was a convalescent but who still had his position as Vice-Consul in Stockholm, heard tell about a kidnap attempt?

Had he been able to arrange for us to be stopped at the border? No, not at all, everything went well and the kidnap victim didn't understand a thing.

It later came to me, that my mother's female instincts must have been quite natural, I had to be part of the deal.

After a stay at auntie Kari's in Ulvik, I ended up at Landøya in Asker, a place Max had bought just after the liberation.

There I lived until I got married. Max turned into uncle Max and a more orderly life took shape, though perhaps not always welcome from my point of view."

Speepy Bird - Jan Arnt

Life

2016

Life -who can describe life?

Is life created by our Lord and is he the one to through dies for us all determining the way we develop as individuals? It looks like that is the situation, when we register how randomly life seems to treat us.

In that case he must possess many dies and a lot of helpers to be able to embrace the entire world's population.

Is it him giving us guidelines to how we best are to live our lives?

When looking at all the misery in the world it is difficult to believe that is the case.

Life has different values in various cultures, and in some it seems like it has no value at all.

Fortunately, we know very little about life apart from that it starts and at an unpredictable time ends.

Another thing we, apart from that know about it is that all of us are living it in one or another way, as long as we stay alive. Most probably we live it as individually different as there are people on this earth, or put in another way as there are different fingerprints.

Some have big ambitions in life while others don't seem conscious of that property at all.

We are all different, arriving from different environment and belonging to different religions.

We live under different climate, belong to different forms of society's and perform different tasks in the society we belong to.

Some claim they are eligible to a larger part of the social benefits than others and claim they deserve it, while others deal with the situation as it is and is happy that way.

Some is in need of showing strength to maintain their self-esteem while others fully obeys rules and regulations drawn up for what's right and wrong.

Others again acts as if they were the ones making the rules and regulations.

We all want to live, or at least most of us.

But when life is on its way to come to an end for whatever reason, and one still is conscious and clear, does one miss something? Specially if it happens at a young age?

One may at that stage not have got the big overview.

Does one ever in life get the big overview, and what may that consist of?

Even if one believe that one have found the answer to the big overview, will there still be something one miss, something one feels undone?

This theme is undoubtedly so personal and meanings so many that it leads nowhere to go further.

Apart from that one should not dwell to much about it either, time comes soon enough when to many of these thoughts are coming to mind.

When that happens it's presumably good, at least for some, to think about the life one have led to live and how one have disposed of it. Because that is life itself.

Is it likely that one ever get the big overview, and will one ever know what one misses?

"What is life, a breath in the sea, which descends……" by Adam Oehlenschlæger, is one most of us have heard about.

Søren Kirkegaard has a wonderful description of life:

"The day you came to the world, you cried while your close ones where happy. Live life so that the day you die, your close ones will cry while you're happy".

Imagine how simple things would be if we stopped worrying.

Samuel Johnson is in his full right stating:

"It's useless to worry about life, you won't get out of it alive anyhow"

I don't know who was the first one with this, but for me it has long time been a good rule of life that:

"Problems do not exist, only challenges".

"Live the life as if you are going to die tomorrow" is a saying. To me this sounds rather dramatic.

Should one fully comply with this rule, one could be personally guilty in one's short stay on mother earth.

If it is correct that most of us agree that life is an art of balance, something at least I advocate for, then maybe my own formulation in various ways illustrates this.

"Life is like a continuous surf. You must keep the balance until you reach land. Only then it's over".

After having written the above it strikes me that I so far only have mentioned life in conjunction with us people- extremely egocentric.

Our lives would of course not have existed if we were the only living creatures on earth.

After all, we are only one form of life among millions.

I am not thinking about life comparable with us, but all form of life needed to keep us humans going.

This is probably too much to comprehend.

We must only accept that we in one or another form are created, that we are a tiny little part of a whole and that all life are dependent of one other.

The following "slogans" used this days in some TV channels, is a reminder in this context.

"If nature is not kept healthy, humans won't survive" and the other from the nature:" If you don't take care of me, I can't take care of you".

Unfortunately, we humans are putting too much load on the nature. Admittedly, at times we pull our self together and try to clean up misery, but only when we realise that we have let it go too far. That however is not good enough.

Maybe it's time we extend our thoughts about life from being egocentric "us selves first", to seriously consider how we, after all having the ability to act, can do something to keep continuous balance in the nature.

It must in this context be added that a big group of us devote themselves to improve our relation to nature which is good if it doesn't become fanatic.

We must never forget that if war breaks out between the nature and us, now doubt we will be the losers. There are plenty of challenges.

In my 78th year I have reached the view that our cycle as individuals on this earth is magnificently adapted to our development.

Through our life we are constantly developing.

If we live long enough we will among others see next generations starting where we left, knowing that they will go through the same development as we did.

I don't believe those advocating that we can learn from experience gained by others.

In life we must all gain experience ourselves, at times in a heavy way, not from others.

Confuse II - Jan Arnt 2010

Light and Shadow

2017

Where you find light consequently you find shadow.

Light can have different strength in the same way as the shadow can have all shades from white to black through the whole spectre.

Thus, opposites like light and shadow is not to be compared with black and white.

The expressions "Like day and night" is used in many contexts.

It is used to pin point, beyond doubt that the case is obvious or, in other words black or white. No question about shades of shadow of any kind seen from the one using the expression.

Those who live materialistically well are often described as those living on the sunny side while, the less privileged often are described like those living on the shadow side of life.

Exactly for the reason of the brightness of light and the spectre of shadows, the phrase after my opinion fits well, as here we don't talk about black and white.

To activate light a switch is needed, and a so called "dimmer", when variety in the strength of light is required.

The "dimmer" is undoubtedly important when looking at the sunny and shadow sides of life.

Is limelight also a form of light which ought to be regulated in intensity?

If that is so I believe no switch is required; typically, an example where the "dimmer" is the best and only solution.

Personally, I have never thought about if I have lived in the shadow of others, but can easily imagine this may have been difficult for those who feel they have.

In this context the spectre of shadows are crucial for how this eventually is felt. For <u>that</u> reason, also here a switch is out of question.

A "dimmer" is obvious, which can display all the spectre of shadows.

All light we experience on earth is created by the sun. All life stretching for the sun receive energy.

Who turned on the switch when the sun was lit? No, along this track we will get nowhere.

Anyhow, no ordinary switch in this case, the nature itself took care of that challenge.

The day the sun quits its lightening, all life we know will probably seize to exist.

A bit gloomy maybe, but as the experts predict it to take some hundred million yeas until it happens, we should not be too much concerned about it.

As we speak about the phrase black and white related to night and day, it should be taken with a pinch of salt. After all, every now and then the moon makes its appearance on the heaven, and what about the stars?

As I understand it, the sun is always standing behind the light. Yeas, literally said. It has hidden behind the sector of the earth where we are as observers. So, in this context, both the moon and the stars reflects the light from the sun without us seeing it directly. In other words, we see the sunlight as a reflex from the moon and the stars.

It's not the sun which has hidden itself, but our little globe orbiting around the sun and around its own axis.

I trust this has been a simple and understanding presentation of light and shadow?

Remember, face the sun and the shadows will always fall behind you

Looking out for number one (version 2)

June 2015

In the first version of "Looking out for number one" which I wrote in October 2013, I took hold of a couple of examples of most people's reaction being confronted with installations which everyone agrees are necessary but mostly dislike to have to close to their environment, as that could feel unpleasant and create consequences in their life.

Furthermore I included an example of the opposite, the pleasure of having an installation within reach, not causing unpleasantness.

The first example deals with wind power and the other high speed trains. It's printed in my book REFLECTIONS II.

In this version of "Looking out for number one", I focus more on our daily reactions.

The reason I get to this now is that I am strongly concerned with the phenomenon "looking out for number one".

It's both natural and obvious that everyone physically is closest to one self. However, that is normally not what we think about when this expression is used.

If we at all have anything in mind in this context, it must be that we in most situations first and foremost think about our self.

In many situations in life I suppose that's only natural and usual. Most probably it must do with self-preservation.

Many will recognize themselves in a variety of daily situations, as most of us would like to be winners, getting the head a little in front of the ones we are surrounded with.

It often feels like only a few have been so fortunate as to have parents which have thought them good manners, and what that means in its widest sense.

They who poses and uses this ability, at least within the family, are today the deviation from the norm, as the only thing that matters is to win, therefore being closest to oneself.

Well, back to the expression.

In the Supermarket, what matters most is to find the line which one think will give the quickest access to the cashier. Quite logical most would say, that's common sense, nothing negative about that as one feel like a winner if one can beat the ones in the other lines.

In this context I suppose women normally pulls the longest straw, as their experience supersede the men in the art of shopping.

Personally I tend to end up in the line that brings me last to the cashier, even if I think I do my calculations in that respect well before deciding in which one to go.

Everyone is closest to him or herself in this context and with a little bit of consciousness one will even avoid hitting the one in front on the Achilles heel with the trolley.

As for parking space, which normally it is too little of, only one thing matters and that is to secure oneself the first available one.

That's only fair if you're not of the polite type which gallantly waves his or her citizen to take the one which obviously is yours.

In this case one goes on compromise with ones winning instincts, very often to great irritation for the drivers behind, which seldom sympathize with such gallantry delaying them in winning.

Even if I add myself the property, in such situations not to be specifically ambitious, I suppose that most of us are closest to ourselves.

Furthermore, I believe more than I make a little battle plan when we enter the gate at an airport, as very few if any of the carriers have found a sustainable solution for the boarding.

The one advising those with seats from row 16 to 32 going first, is only one not functioning, as all passengers are closest to themselves pressing on in the hope to win the fight about the overhead compartment.

My best experience related to this subject I got not to long time ago during a trip from Istanbul to Madrid with Turkish Airlines. At the gate, they had made three separated rows numbered 1- 2- and 3. When I too late discovered that each row had a corresponding reference on the boarding card, I ended of course up in the back of my row.

Anyway, this is so far the best example I have seen.

Next time I Fly Turkish Airways, if it will ever happen, I will remember this arrangement with pleasure.

All this of course doesn't matter if one has ordered business or first class, but that is logically limited to some few.

It's on its place to mention that these days I travel much less than earlier years, and thereby may have been lacking behind when keeping track with development.

However, irrespective of system, most of us will probably by intuition look for a short cut, as we are closest to ourselves.

Have these examples to do with egoism and in that case, not only for our self but also for our close ones?

What if we didn't have this drive to be closest to ourselves - would the society function better, would it be better flow in the lines and would we be less stressed?

Open mouth - Jan Arnt 2010

Love

2015

This heading has remained empty for a long time, a very long time. Not because I couldn't get started on it but, and that's most likely my explanation in a nutshell, because love is probably the world's most significant word, a word one ought to have the greatest respect for.

One can't get started on a reflection about love just like that.

Practically all types of literature is concerned, at least partly, with love.

Normally not only with the simple emotional attraction between individual people but often with the one lightly seasoned with the sensual. The sometimes almost animal attraction, can create a suspense which makes the reader concentrate. I'll put this part which is of course important, but which is far from being all that love has to offer, behind me first.

I'll never forget my first contact with the literary insight into the matter.

In the bookcase on the far wall of the sitting room in the "old" house at Landøya where I grew up, about a metre away from the keyboard of the grand piano, was the book: "Lady Chatterley's Lover".

The word love I couldn't at that time the book was published in Norwegian in 1952 when I was about thirteen, really relate to of course. Even though I have no memory of it, I must somehow have had an understanding of the word, but I can't remember growing up with any special warmth from being spoiled with love. Nor was the opposite in any way the case, but I probably saw myself as someone who had fallen between two stools in one form or other.

Nothing wrong with having a stepfather as such, but perhaps there wasn't quite enough room for all three of us at the beginning during those postwar days.

Anyway, the book became, as with millions of other readers, my first literary contact with sexual matters and we'll leave it at that.

The sexual part of love I learnt to understand early on, whereas the part related to its combination with deeper feelings took somewhat longer.

It must have been a copy of the first edition of the book in Norwegian that they had in their bookcase. As far as I remember, it was illustrated with drawings, albeit without any erotic angle, as I recall.

As it at times was carefully being coaxed out of the bookcase for a closer acquaintance, it was always put back with the greatest of care, so that its having been "borrowed" wouldn't be discovered.

At approximately the same time, I seem to recall that the pornographic magazine "Cocktail" caused great excitement, when one on rare occasions came across a copy.

It might, of course, be tempting to continue along this track, but where should I then draw the line. It could well be that I in that case would get carried away, which would undoubtedly lead me astray, as there is definitely more to love than the erotic.

As mentioned above, it took somewhat longer to gain an understanding of its combination with the deeper feelings of love, and there is really no reason why I should know something which others don't about the word love, which in my opinion is the most important one in our vocabulary.

It is just great to look up its various definitions, and there are lots of them when it comes to love. The love of whom of what and its various forms is described in detail which, of course isn't strange when one thinks of the significance of love. In practically all forms of literature love is present and where it appears, it is given special attention.

Without being able to put my finger on it, I believe it's just as important to be able to give as to be able to receive love; and here, as in so many other situations in life, it's a question of balance.

I'm probably skating on thin ice here. To give and receive in this case, as far as love goes, won't seem as right and true if there's talk about conscious control, in other words if it's all about determination and not feeling, will it?

No wonder the topic is a complicated one.

Love between two people is in my opinion unreservedly dependent on honesty, tolerance and respect for one another, if the relationship is to function.

This I have long since been convinced of and thus I quote in reversed order, an excerpt from a speech I made to my nephew, Thomas, and his, Trine, on their wedding day the 6th of August, 2005.

"Respect for one another:
A well-known and important expression which is far-reaching as well as being an extremely important ingredient in dealing with the many challenges of married life.

The good thing is that one doesn't need any experience in order to respect one another. Here all one needs is awareness. Reminding oneself from time to time what having respect for one another means in its broadest sense and acting accordingly.

Tolerance:
This word stands for patience and the acceptance of other people's opinions.

Where the ceiling is high, the volume is always greater and there's more room to play.

Opposites attract it is said and there's probably a lot of truth in that, but not without tolerance.

Honesty:

Honesty is also not to be frowned upon. Suspicion and jealousy are poison and can be hidden dangers on the road of life. If one makes honesty part of one's daily agenda, as well as a good portion of tolerance and respect for one another, many of life's sharp edges can be blunted.

Love, last but not least:
Saying that I love you is allowed. Nor is it forbidden to say it several times a day. Can that really be necessary, some of you may ask, we are married after all, so it must go without saying. Fact is, it doesn't go without saying. We need all the encouragement we can get from these three words and it

always does one good to hear them, preferably several times a day".

For me, the touch of love is important.

To hold a hand, to touch and feel contact.

I have often said that I should have been a carpenter. I love working with wood, also being there at the beginning, cutting down a tree.

This always happens with the greatest of respects as the most important growth in nature is undoubtedly just that, the tree, if one excludes the nutritious plants needed in order for human beings and animals to exist, that is.

Love of things is also a form of love. If it weren't for the tree, it would have been so-so with most things in society. The most important base element in earlier construction, apart from stone, must have been wood. How could our forefathers have been able to construct the most important means of communication, the boat, if the tree hadn't existed? Development would have taken infinitely longer, which would have meant that the world today would have looked completely different.

Thor Heyerdal with, Kon Tiki, his raft made of balsa, and his reed boat, Ra, proved without a doubt that communication can have happened that way, in other words, with the aid of a balsa raft and a reed boat, but the big question is, if there weren't any other clever souls who earlier on understood the importance of wood in this context? We'll leave that hanging in the air.

Perhaps the best one about love between people is the expression which says:

"It falls as easily on a turd as on a lily".

Love is the food of life.

Occurrence

April 2014

In short, a person's perception of an occurrence is the content of his or her subjective experience.

Subjectivity indicates bias and partiality, in other words, the opposite of objectivity, whereas experience is the knowledge one gains from occurrences. I must admit that I don't quite understand where bias enters into it as regards subjectivity, but I expect you'll have a clearer picture of it.

If I continue, it'll easily become more confusing, so I'll stick with the short version. The fact is that further explanation forces you to go more deeply into things and then the terms become somewhat unclear, at least for me. An occurrence, the way we experience it, is really quite simple, isn't it?

What is it then, that characterizes an occurrence and what are the criteria which turn a subjective experience, which I see as a form of event, into a special occurrence?

In my opinion an event hasn't got any characteristics, nor do I believe that there are certain criteria which define an occurrence, perhaps one can say that an occurrence is a special event, an extraordinary one, or are all events occurrences?

My simple answer to that question is that an occurrence becomes that which each of us turns an event into.

For each individual it is thus entirely possible to turn the smallest event into a special occurrence, in fact, even a great one.

Many seem to have understood this, probably unconsciously, as some have the ability never to keep the most uninteresting events to themselves. They are frequently referred to with great gusto by the person concerned and are often characterized as great occurrences.

What is not so good is that people with this ability often have the habit of repeating the stories of said events over and over again.

I believe most of us can refer to occurrences of this type.

Regardless, to be fair, trifling occurrences can for some seem incredibly important, in which case they become valuable to the person concerned and not trifling.

Near death occurrences are, according to Wikipedia, experiences which are sometimes described by those who have been near death, or who have been clinically dead before returning to life. These experiences are often interpreted as showing that there is life after death.

Enough said, occurrences are experienced by everyone, regardless of gender or background, throughout life.

Occurrences normally appear in two main groups, the good ones and the bad ones, and we can only hope that for most of us, there are more of the first category than the second.

With the millions of people travelling every year, one would think that travel events constitute a large part of people's occurrences.

This, however, must once again be an individual matter if we agree that for each and every one of us, a special occurrence is what one turns an event into.

Just imagine the kind of freedom it gives you to be able to determine your own occurrences.

If it's great or small, or spans over a shorter or a longer period; one we've experienced on our own or one we've shared with others. It doesn't matter, what matters is that it is our very own special occurrence.

For me the most important occurrences are those I can share with others.

My wife's birthday has been on the 29th of July every year so far in her life and this date arrives naturally enough on different days of the week.

A few years ago we were going on a trip to Copenhagen. I had various meetings on Monday the 30th, so we had booked plane tickets for Saturday the 28th. The only departure was in the evening around half past seven.

The plane is on time and we arrive at the Radisson Blue Royal Hotel, in the centre of Copenhagen at about half past eleven.

When we got to our room on the eighteenth floor, with a view of the Tivoli, I ordered a bottle of red wine and some cheese. It had nothing to do with saving money that it wasn't Champagne, but we both prefer red wine with cheese.

The bottle arrived along with a simple selection of cheeses.

The Tivoli is still full of people just before closing time and beautifully lit. I look at my watch which shows that we are getting close, then pour the wine and get ready for the birthday toast.

At twelve on the dot, the famous and magnificent fireworks of the Tivoli, which goes off every Saturday night in the season, starts.

The normally black sky is lit as if it were in the middle of a sunny day.

In silence we watch the séance, which I reckon last around ten minutes, whereupon I lift my glass and toast another year in the logbook.

My wife has hardly recovered from the shock before I, with mock modesty say: "that's the least I can do for my darling on her birthday".

A wonderful occurrence.

Goldfish - Jan Arnt 2010

Poem of Joy

The greatest joy of all must be,
others smiling and laughing to see.
That others can feel what in life is real.

There are enough days when thoughts are bad
and enough of them when thoughts are sad.

But the thoughts full of joy can themselves fill a book,
it's just a question of knowing where to look.

Keep your eyes open and your vision clear,
take care of beauty, it's extremely dear.

Look after that which us feeds
and don't hide away in the reeds.

Because although each straw is thin and brittle,
together their density makes you feel little.

You can't find the exit, you grope around rather,
you clutch at the air, is that what you gather?

A mountain of straw can't be climbed by force,
you have to make use of life's spiritual source.

You must lift yourself up and release your juices,
you must want to and let your force have its uses.

You've got the necessary strength,
it's just a question until what length.

You can score your points, one after the other,
make your decision, repeat, it's no bother.

Do it for ever, be on the alert,
and you'll never be bitter and hurt.

January 1995 (Cabrera)

Pride

May 2014

"It's nothing to be proud of", or the opposite "I'm proud of you" or "You can be proud of that", are expressions one pays attention to, particularly if they come from someone with authority in one area or another, and applies to one self.

It's something about being careful before contacting someone with the expression "It's nothing to be proud of".

One should in advance have a thoughtful reason for doing so. Nothing is more hurtful than if the accusation being the basis for using the expression is incorrect and only based on assumptions and rumours.

If you receive the expression "It's nothing to be proud of" from someone, think carefully before you answer.

Maybe the right thing to do is to test oneself every now and then. How would I react if someone in one way or another told me that: "It's nothing to be proud of"?

If someone address themselves with the expression: "I'm proud of you", and one knows it's well meant, one feel the warmth.

Being honest, which one of course is, newer use the expression "I am proud of you" to anyone, unless you mean it full heartedly.

We know it is warming when someone use that expression to us, and we know it is well meant and deserved.

However, if one feel that it's not honestly meant, maybe more sarcastic, it can sear quite strongly.

Maybe one should tidy up one's own use of this types of compliments.

How often do you yourself use this last expression: "I'm proud of you"?

Think about how you would react if you from someone that means a lot to you should receive these four words, wouldn't it warm you?

Pride shines out of the eyes, the purpose is achieved.

The goal is achieved. The bigger the offer has been and the more you have sacrificed to reach the goal, the prouder you are.

I think we have all been acquainted with the good feeling of pride.

This type of pride is just as big whatever the case. It's not a matter about the size of the feats.

Every ting is personal and proportional.

It being the first balance on the bike, the distinction one got in sport or other milestones, the pride is personal and proportional with the importance of the efforts to reach the goal.

The most important pride is the one on behalf of others.

It gives double pleasure, especially if one has been personally part of that which the one in question deserve the expression for. "You can be proud of that".

We all have a hint of personal pride, and that's both right and important.

When this type of pride gets overdeveloped it becomes difficult to deal with.

With overdeveloped personality it feels good to express that one is proud of what one has done.

It's often the way the pride is expressed which matters.

"Modesty is a virtue" is an expression.

Does one act with superior attitude because one is afraid of making a fool of oneself, or to expose oneself?

Has it something to do with taking oneself to serious?

The personal pride should not be overdeveloped

In my opinion the most sympathetic pride is the one shown on behalf of others – but it must be honest.

Regret

2015

Those who know what they are talking about, as to have an emotional answer to one's physiological reaction on being offended, denied something or done unjust. To regret, often releases when one's borders are threatened. Some have a thought tendency to react on regret with revenge.

Most probably we all feel instinctively what is meant by regretting something, and it would be strange if not all of us could find personal examples related to this. For myself I make the matter of regretting, a definitive case. Either you regret something you have done, or you regret something you have said ore written.

To regret something you have done, may often set big marks and give consequences which are irrevocable, while to regret something you have not done, in most cases may give you a kind of desire, but normally something one can easily accept to live with.

About regrets, I wrote some words in 1994, which I think covers my attitude to this.

> I regret very little of what I have done
> as luckily my memory's quickly gone.
> I regret more what I didn't get done,
> all of which would have been second to none.
> Gave people a chance – from near and far,
> always kept the door ajar.
> Yes, it has often been very dear
> and hasn't always got out of low gear.
> A tougher stand with demands and decision -
> would that have been the answer to greater expansion?
> Undoubtedly short term but wherein lies the strength,
> in those who know their profession at length.
> One needs practical experience and time to roost,
> maturity, effort and lots of boost.

By instinct one knows immediately that something one has said, preferably should stay unsaid. As a rule, it is too late to regret, and consequences follows

In my youth, I hope I have grown better as years have passed by, I think I was more than normally big mouthed. We have all got our ways to stand out I suppose. All the way back to those days, when I was seventeen I still bear with me one terrible example of something I said. It could never be erased, however much I would have liked it to be. The episode is to grim to present here, but I only mention this because I am convinced that I am not alone having this kind of thoughts. Also because to regret in this way can be felt as hurting badly.

Next follows two short rimes I put on paper many years ago, and I hope they can serve as a reminder to someone.

Gossip

The words that wander from mouth to ear -
can for some be sad to hear.
So let the thoughts in your mind go around,
before you put them to paper or sound.

To paper

When one puts to paper what one thinks and means -
it can be interpreted wrongly and lead to scenes.
Now, no one must ever think that what one eventually regrets,
will disappear by one setting some words on paper as a way to make up.
So easy it is not, and should of course not be.
If one however, daily, is a little more conscious in one`s where about,
I believe that one can reduce one`s anger-account and thereby make one`s
life more easy to live.

Revolution

2017

Revolution is a mouth full to grab hold of. The word revolution originates from the Latin "revolutio" which means upheavals. Wikipedia explains it as follows: A concept used about a fundamental change process taking place over a short period of time.

This I will set aside, as I don't qualify to go deeper into the subject so wide reaching and so confusing.

Short and sweet, I look at revolution as the reverse of evolution which in Latin is "evolutio".

When it comes to evolution it is not expected that the development happens fast and in big steps, on the contrary.

Many talks about revolutionary technical developments and those there have been masses of since I was born in 1939 and up to today.

It is possible that I am astray, but if one by revolutionary technical developments accepts that the development goes over time, in this case not more than 125 years I may still be on the right track.

I feel I have been lucky and privileged to be joining a special voyage in this context, in the period from immediately after the last world war in 1945 and until today.

In that period I didn't only sit on the side line, but in all modesty took part in the revolution itself. It is all about 60 years of development of the concept "from speech to text", or said in other words, "where speech is converted to text".

It all started with Thomas Edison`s invention of the so called "Phonograph" back in 1877, where one could store sound for later to listen to the content. The invention gave way to development of a series of practical machines, among other the record player and much later in time, in 1923, the dictating machine.

The American Company Dictaphone was most probably the first to introduce Edison's solution of storing and retrieving speech for practical use in dictation and transcribing.

In 2016 it was 7 decades since my stepfather's first operational year in the office machine business in Norway, together with his partner Sophus Clausen in the company they formed together, Clausen & Manus Kontormaskiner. (Office machines)

The first representation for dictating machines they got hold of was the Dictaphone machines. The sound media used in these machines at the time was wax rollers and they had to be grinded after use, if to be used again.

In practical terms this meant that Clausen & Manus Kontormaskiner did sell and service dictating machines from the first time they where introduced on the Nordic markets and being substantially used in offices of all kind.

As time went by all types of sound media saw daylight and many countries produced dictating machines.

Continually new technological innovations took place and little was left untried related to improve the dictating machine, without me going into details about that.

As for the sound media one did go for a variety of choices such as steel wire, magnetic disks, magnetic rollers, belts, cuffs and magnetic tapes of various types.

Sophus Clausen and Max split as partners in 1952. They also negotiated a split of agencies, and Max formed his own company Max Manus Kontormaskiner.

As for dictating machines, Sophus kept Dictaphone, and as Max also wanted to stay in that field as well, he soon after got hold of the German agency Stenocord.

At that time, both Dictaphone and Stenocord used magnetic belts, also called cuffs.

Dictating machines had already become an important part of the office administration both in the private and public sector.

Philips came on the market with its first dictating machine in 1957. It was based on magnetic tape as sound media, but with a drastic difference from earlier magnetic tape machines. The difference being that both the ribbon coils, the full and the empty, was assembled in a closed cassette.

This way the treatment and the ease of use became dramatically better when compared with existing magnetic tape machines.

In 1957-58 Max Manus Kontormaskiner got the representation for Philips dictating machines, first in Norway and then Denmark, and soon grabbed a solid market share.

When Philips invented the so called Minicassette and introduced them in their machines, they soon became market leaders.

By time the PC entered the marked it soon took over the work of most traditional office machines. No one listened any more to the argument that one dictates 7 times faster than one writes. More and more people started writing themselves, a trend it was not possible, nor correct to fight against.

Large users of dictating machines, such as Hospitals and Lawyers however, continued using the most rational method at that time converting speech to text, dictating machine and transcription by secretary. Transcription was gradually made with transition from manual and electric typewriters, to PCs.

If the heavy users did not show a continues demand for transfer of speech to text, it would be doubtful if continuous product development would have happened the way it did.

Max Manus Forskning AS (Research) with Bjørn Andersen at the steering wheel, conducted for more than 40 years among other, development of loud-speaking intercom systems.

I had the great pleasure of having a close and good cooperation with him throughout all this years.

Philips intercom as these products where named, gave us valuable market feed-back, and as the Hospitals already since the 1960 and until new revolutionary solutions within speech processing entered the market in the first part of 2000, it became only logical for our research company to take the challenge of developing a combined system for dictation, transcription and speech communication.

The finished product which we called DICOM 2010, was supplied to more than 150 hospitals in Norway and Denmark, with many thousand users and was probably the most advanced ever manufactured.

During this exciting times quite a few companies in the world was developing speech-recognition, which means automatically converting speech to text by means of technical aids.

As with all form of technological breakthroughs, all parties involved in this type of development did not have an easy time, but in the latter part of 1990, everyone in the field knew it was only a matter of time until speech-recognition would become a practical reality.

This challenge the third generation in Max Manus AS took charge of, with a great deal of enthusiasm and success.

Based on products from Philips and later Nuance, Max Manus AS was the company bringing speech-recognition to users in Norway and Denmark.

In 2005 the first speech-recognition system was delivered to a Norwegian hospital, and during the following years these systems became standard in hospitals.

Today speech-recognition is almost covering the total Hospital market in Norway.

Introduction of this new technology took longer time in Denmark, but from 2009 we were also there well on the way.

Max Manus AB in Sweden was established in 2010, and the introduction on that market has proven to be a challenging effort until now.

For more than a decade, Max Manus AS have developed speech-recognition integration modules for a series of different hospital systems, and this days we are supplying our own developed, complete Norwegian speech-recognition system for general use which, hopefully will find its way to a variety of users in the society.

No one can with accuracy tell which way the development will lead us, but as one will understand, I feel in all modesty that I have had the privilege of being part of an exciting technical revolutionary voyage during the last 60 years.

"From dictation to a wax cylinder and transcription by means of typewriter – to speech-recognition where the speech automatically is converted to text"

Rigoletto

June 2014

Most will recognize the title as being the name of the opera written in 1851 by the Italian opera composer Guiseppe Verdi.

Well, this reflection has, as one will soon understand no resemblance with the opera Rigoletto. The scene is a shiny white Triumph TR6 1970 model with the canopy folded, which in 50 kph, and squished as far to the right on the road as possible to allow all other traffic to pass.

On top of the canopy my wife to be is sitting, clinging to a Yucca palm raising almost tree meters between her legs.

She became my wife in ninety-eight, two years later.

The diameter of the trunk itself was not even five centimetres, and although the leaves on the top were not many and big, the air forces the bush against her with great force.

As she is not built large and heavy, she used all her force to keep the new purchase in a vertical position.

As I am driving I sit on the left side in the front. The car is British, but originally built for the American market, thus the left-hand drive.

Even if the speed isn't great, her blond hair blows in the wind while cars races by in both directions.

Every now and then we are passed by large trucks using this rode from the harbour in Garrucha to the Plaster mines in Sorbas to collect cargo.

Horns are honking every time a lorry overtake us, while the drivers laughs and shouts enthusiastic comments.

We have collected the palm at the garden centre Haro, and are on our way home to Cabrera to plant it on a place suitable for the purpose on the terrace.

The stretch we drive while the lorries overtakes us is about five kilometres, where after we take off for our local village Turre.

From there it's another six kilometres up to Cabrera and to our house, situated exactly four hundred meter above sea level.

This event took place a spring day in ninety six and we had just moved into the house.

Unfortunately, no pictures were taken, nor from the transport or the planting, but as this episode took place more than 20 years ago, a camera would be needed, as the mobile with this function built in, was not yet available.

The road from Turre up to Cabrera, was in those days quite narrow. Apart from a few stretches, if two cars met each other, one had to stop to let the other pass.

Also on this local stretch we heard a few supportive and enthusiastic shouts and laughter's.

Finally outside the garage, the challenge was to get it the 52 stairs up through the lift shaft, to reach the terraces outside the house.

The lift was not yet installed, but even if it had been it could not make place for the Yucca palm.

We had already decided where to plant it and had prepared for it.

After quite some struggle we got it to the terrace and planted.

When finally in the ground, watered and well anchored in its new environment, the glass of white vine to celebrate tasted specially good in the afternoon sun.

Maybe it was the special transport that gave us so close contact with the new acquisition that we decided it deserved its own name.

My wife is from Switzerland and Genève and has French as her mother thong. She thought the trip from Haro had been the most unusual and exiting car trip she had ever had, and particularly she had fancied the laughter, shouts and enthusiastic comments.

To Laugh in French is "Rigoler", something I didn't know until she told me.

No further polemic. There and then we decided that the child should be named "Rigoletto".

With a ceremoniously toast I proclaimed, at the same time as giving it an extra spray of water, that it should be named "Rigoletto".

During the same period a lot of plants and trees were planted both around the terrace and what we called the garden outside the house.

The reason for the lift tower to be built is that it's the only entrance to the house, which is built on the top of a more than ten meter high outcrop, not much larger than the house itself.

The view is fantastic.

To the Vest, in good weather one can see the snow mountains in Sierra Nevada, and to the East, in a clear night, the light tower in Cartagena.

Marianne and I married in 1998 and spent our first ten years in the house in Cabrera.

After a while the lift was installed, and parallel to us entering "The Vintage age" that of course became a relief.

"Rigoletto" adapted itself perfectly, and grew with a speed not to be believed.

The one little trunk my wife held on to when we collected it, soon became tree, which as time went by had to be trimmed when they started fighting the strong winds that at times can occur above the ceiling of the house.

Maybe it also flourished thanks to the music we always plaid on the terrace, we never know.

Around 2006 we came to the conclusion that the house in Cabrera became too much to deal with, both regarding the driving up and down as well as everything to do with the up-keeping.

We were well into our seven-tees and felt that life could easier be lived in a small flat adapted to our needs.

We ended up around 25 minutes' drive from Cabrera, on what we call the flat land. Not because it's flat, but because it's surrounded by mountains on all sides apart from towards the Mediterranean See.

This gives us a good balance between our "Vintage age" and the daily challenges.

"Rigoletto" is still going strong. Each of the tree trunks has, at their lowest part, a waist of around 150 cm.

Now doubt it thrives, where it stands with its green painted fields where trunks have been trimmed to avoid them to grow to dominant.

Stubbornness

May 2012

I won't immediately characterize stubbornness as a disease in line with what I believe extreme jealousy to be. Here as elsewhere there are many degrees and nuances.

The simple well-known form of stubbornness which everyone possesses and at times applies, is of a relatively innocent character.

In fact it can be both humorous and charming and is part of everyone's daily life and relationships.

We can also skip lightly over the kind of stubbornness children use to attract attention. That's a gift of nature and a prerequisite for development. It's not in any way damaging but has, of course, a strong impact on the child's upbringing.

If the cry is honoured repeatedly to achieve family peace it says itself that one is doing the wrong thing, but it's clear here as elsewhere that one has to find a balance.

As we know, black and white is not always a viable alternative. Perhaps it seems the most simple, but it is in no way the most character building.

We can probably all agree on what has been said so far, one has to add a bit of spice to everyday life in order to make things work.

It is worse when someone's stubbornness becomes a kind of obsession, turning towards the fanatical. Against all odds and common sense and with a total lack of logic and sense of reality, a lot of people forge ahead without considering the turbulence they're causing when dealing with others who in the given context react normally and use these very senses to navigate through the waters of everyday life.

It is especially bad for people with a strong sense of fairness. Everything turns upside down when normal values are set aside by such brutal and illogical means.

The result is unfortunately quite often a temporary break in communication or worse.

Total resignation is felt by the affected party whilst the initiator with his or her extreme variety of stubbornness moves on through life as if nothing has happened.

One has to ask oneself if it's actually possible for someone to be so removed from reality that they have no idea of what they've started.

Or could it be that they feel that it's a means, with a bit of luck, to achieving changes in conditions, things or situations?

Both are probably adequate reasons.

Wouldn't it be easy for those affected to think, oh well, this is so crazy that we'll just let it go, take it all with a smile and defuse the situation?

Those who recognize themselves will probably say that they have, of course, tried it that way, but there are limits to how far one can stretch when the situation repeats itself several times in a row over a long period of time.

Those who have managed to read this far probably ask themselves if the writer of these words can refer to his own frightening examples of stubbornness, and I can assure you he can.

Headache - Jan Arnt 2010

Summer Job

May 2013

If one had the possibility of getting a summer job, and I believe most of us did back in the early fifties, it certainly came in handy.

Pocket money was in short supply at least in my case.

Not that my parents couldn't afford it but I believe part of their idea of upbringing was that one should give in order to get.

Everything has, of course, a balance, but I have to say that I partly agree with my parents' restraint, even though I didn't really adhere to their principles when my daughters were growing up, but then those were entirely different times.

It also wasn't too difficult for my step-father, Max, to give me various tasks to do for the firm.

The first few years I got a ride to the office with my mother and Max. We lived on Landøya in Asker, eighteen kilometres from Oslo. My mother was Max's secretary at the time and the firm's head office was situated in Karl Johans gate 21.

Errand boy is probably a long gone profession, but at the time it was part of the running of a firm. The work in my case meant carrying stacks of invoices and delivering them to the customers in question for payment. It had nothing to do with the customers being late payers, it was, as far as I recall, only part of the routine. It sometimes happened that the invoices were paid this way, that is to say by personal visits, but that was, if I remember correctly, only sporadically.

A bit more exciting was the job of wax cylinder changer. Since the firm was the agent in Norway for the American Dictaphone dictation machines after the war, this was part of the running of these.

The machines were based on the use of wax cylinders which had to be sanded down after use in order to be reused. The customers had subscriptions saying that the cylinders were to be picked up and redelivered at certain times. I believe I went around with a specially made stand which could be filled up with these wax cylinders. Oh well, that's the way it worked in the technical stone age of those days.

I was from an early age technically inclined and at fourteen a friend of mine and I experimented with making self-sealing envelopes. These had apparently not yet been invented or we, at least, hadn't heard of them or seen them being used. My friend worked the chemical side of things, that is with the glue or adhesive, whereas I was in charge of the mechanical part which would automatically apply it to the envelopes. We had, of course, no way of reaching industrial results, but there was no lack of enthusiasm and commitment. The envelopes ended up working just fine.

The paper-clip is in itself a significant invention but for some reason, and I have no idea what triggered me, I felt it should be electrified. Imagine, electrified paper-clips in those days?

Well, it was to work perfectly well and consisted of two cogwheels which fit together. A small switch started the motor which drove them when one inserted the paper corners between the cogwheels. The machine was stationary and attached to the desk so that one always knew where it was.

The perforation of the paper which took place between the two cogwheels when they turned, made the papers stick together. I have strangely enough never seen this idea industrialized so perhaps it wasn't such a good one after all.

The paper-clip incident first saw the light of day after I, also doing a summer job and according to my own wish, was transferred to our office machine workshop, which at the time was situated at Hammersborg square in Oslo.

There was no longer a question of my being given a ride, the workday at the workshop started at seven in the morning in those days, whereas the office opened at nine.

It was all very exciting apart from the bus ride from Landøya to Oslo, leaving at six in the morning.

My part of the work consisted mainly of cleaning calculators and typewriters. First they had to be prepared by removing covers and sensitive parts, such as those made of rubber.

After that the machine was lowered into a solution of spirits where-after special brushes were used to remove lubricants. Then it was dried using an air pressure gun and various types of lubricants were added to moving parts. The removed parts were reinstalled and the machine was tested.

At that time there was talk about all electrical office machines marketed in Norway having to be modified in order to adapt to the Norwegian requirements for "safety" when it came to things like electrical disturbances; so-called noise filters had to be installed.

These modifications were in our workshop done as piecework and often outside of normal working hours if there was a lot to do. One put oneself down for these jobs which were quite popular and which gave one a good extra income, if one worked hard at it. Because mine was a summer job and most of the mechanics wanted to make use of the long summer evenings, I had no problem getting the work.

No complaints about our mechanics, at least not from a summer job worker like me, but I soon saw that they modified each and every machine separately. Tools back and forth, changing drill bits and threading tools, etc.

I found this at once to be very cumbersome and thus the conveyor belt was invented at Max Manus. I put up a long table and placed ten or twenty machines, depending on type, all along it. Then I worked down the row from A to Z with the tool applicable to the various tasks. This way the time it took to work on each machine was reduced to a third, so I made good money.

The conveyor belt technique was rapidly adopted by everyone and after a while the works manager reduced the piecework rate as everything went a bit too smoothly. It was a wonderful time while it lasted, not only because of the modification of the machines and the money it paid, but also because the atmosphere of the workshop was inspiring.

The works manager at the time was a modest man, not especially tall of stature, but as I recall, a great personality in his own way. He earned respect thanks to his personality not his status. I remember it being said that he was once sent on a technical calculator course in France. Not that that in itself is significant, but I believe the machines were produced in Italy, went under the name of Lagomarsino and that we represented them in Norway.

He had apparently not been outside Norway earlier and was not very versed in languages.

It was said that he lost several kilos in a fortnight, his already being slim and as previously mentioned not very tall, because he had problems ordering potatoes in French.

The man, whose name by the way was, Kolbein Lauring, was a close friend and collaborator of Max's during the war and showed himself to be extremely brave in many situations, especially once when he shot his way out of his house while it was surrounded by Germans who had come to arrest him.

It was probably based on these summer jobs and the high requirements the technical education of our mechanics called for, that I at the age of seventeen was employed by the firm and sent to Olivetti's school in Italy to be trained as a technical instructor.

I remained almost two years in Italy, divided between a technical school in Ivrea, Olivetti's headquarters in the North of Italy and a commercial school in Florence.

After my stay, which was, of course, an experience of a life time, I set off home again, where I took over the responsibility for the training of the firm's technical personnel, including the technicians in our five subsidiaries and some thirty dealerships spread throughout the country.

Swallows Nests

June 2012

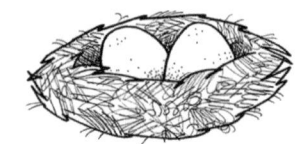

I go straight into plural as I've never seen just one swallows nest, they're always built in clusters.

Having had a chance to establish themselves, the swallows return every year as surely as spring itself. Some architects seem to be experts on swallows or, more clearly put, they design swallow-friendly houses, whereas others seem to know the secret of how to avoid them.

The Spanish architect having designed our complex, who seems to be well-known for his house designs in general, has shown himself to be of the former kind, the swallow-friendly one.

We bought the flat we are living in about three years ago. The twenty-four dwellings in the complex had just been completed when we moved in. The flat is on the first floor and thus one of the top ones in a section of four. Two at ground level and two above, with a view of the thirteenth hole of the golf course.

The sloping tile-covered roof forms an overhang above and beside our front door about three to four meters wide.

Due to the sloping roof the swallows have to duck below the bottom part of this to get to their favourite "construction" site. In other words, the nest is situated where the roof meets the wall, completely protected against wind and bad weather and other enemies as well, be it four-legged ones or others of the bird species.

Already the first spring we were living here, it became clear that we were facing a problem. A problem in the sense that having a swallows nest directly above the front door and more than one in a width of a few meters, is not just a question of having to put up with the continuous twittering of birds, but also of having to clean up the residents continuous leavings.

The situation is impossible. Having come to the conclusion that this can't be accepted, what does one do?

Since we in our first year didn't have any experience with swallows nests, we let them, with some doubt, build their nest in the section beyond the door.

The swallows' attempts to build their nest directly above the door were stopped by continuously demolishing their smallest attempts at securing their "foundation" to the corner.

What we didn't understand was that these individuals are driven by nature and not common sense.

Had we humans had the same amount of determination, ability to work and stamina, many of our challenges would have been avoided.

Common sense or rather the lack of same is the mental barrier for these poor two-winged individuals. They never give up, are probably frustrated, but keep going undauntedly every single day until their season is over.

What they attach to the wall, we take down just as quickly, in their attempt to build a nest above the front door.

It was with great anguish that we watched their hopeless battle.

On the gable wall of our flat we've been observing another battle. A couple of swallows started building a nest there about a month ago, but two sparrows seemed to think that this was their territory. They made an incredible racket during the entire building period without making the swallows give up. The construction was finally finished, but to our astonishment the swallows never moved in. We are now well into May, the sparrows are staying under a roof tile not far from the swallows nest, which remains empty.

The sparrows obviously won the battle with their endurance tactics. Now it's quite peaceful and though the nest wouldn't directly affect our terrace, we're grateful for the help of the sparrows.

Their song is also not so shrill, but as its discrimination to make a judgement based on song quality, it becomes subjective and thus has nothing to do with the matter at hand.

We have tried everything from varnish-like surface paint to various types of chemicals, though nothing hazardous, but there doesn't seem to be anything which will change the building habits of the swallows.

Both my wife and I are animal-lovers and definitely don't want to harm any birds, but there are times when one can't compromise.

The swallows have probably been on this earth as long as humans and we thus ask ourselves: where did they build their nests when people lived in caves and until such time as the swallow-friendly architects came on the scene with their creativity?

The food chain - Jan Arnt 2010

The Architect

Jan. 2015

Luis Collarte Rodriguez was born in Orense in Galicia in 1960. He's an architect and the reason I draw attention to his name in this case is that he was the one who designed the new Parador Hotel Atlantico in the city of Cadiz in Andalucia in Spain.

That it happens to be this particular architect who is taken to task here is not because he's unique in his genre, as this reflection has nothing to do with the design of the building as far as its appearance goes, but because I believe that the perception of most of the customers, as regards the practical outfitting of the rooms, must be like mine, about the worst they've ever seen.

In all fairness, I have to say that I haven't looked into whether or not he is responsible for the design and practical décor of the rooms. If he's not, I can only apologize for his having to bear the brunt. He ought to in future, if he were to design other hotels, really pull up his socks, as he would otherwise, in my opinion, end up with a bad reputation.

If he himself is responsible, however, his shoulders are probably broad enough, for him to ignore the bite of this tiny mosquito.

My wife and I have stayed at the Parador Atlantico in Cadiz on several occasions. We like the old part of the city very much and have lots of good memories from there.

The hotel is perfectly situated with a view of the entrance into the city harbour.

Christmas 2014 was in every way as pleasant as our previous visits but, as indicated above, with some quite unique and surprising observations.

We have, of course, booked a room in advance and arrive as usual by car, after having spent an evening with good friends, staying overnight at Hotel Don Carlos in Marbella. It has taken us about three and a half hours to get from our home to Marbella.

We had heard that the Parador hotel in Cadiz had been renovated, but not

103

that the old one had been torn down and a new one had been built, so the first question we asked ourselves, when we got to the place where we seemed to remember that the hotel ought to be, was if we had completely lost our minds.

This had to be where the hotel was. After having driven past, turned around and once again driven past where we thought the hotel ought to be, we spotted the sign. In the exact place where the old one had been, a new super modern building had been put up.

No comments about the construction nor about the impression the lobby made on us. Everything was in line with what we associate with an elegant modern hotel.

It also makes very impressive reading that the new hotel was built in no more than eighteen months, so there are no negative comments about that, especially when we, after having read the presentation, understand that it was the architect's first designed building. Earlier on he has with great skill worked with important restorations in Leon and Santiago de Compostela, we are given to understand.

The room as such is super modern with a beautiful view toward the Cadiz harbour entrance as well as of a large botanical park and it has a very airy terrace with a glass railing. We are to stay on the seventh floor.

As we get inside the door, it seems natural to move to the left, almost as if by magnetic influence.

A soot coloured wall covered in mirrors about one metre into the room could easily have lead to a serious collision. A mere bagatelle, of course, as it is a mistake one would probably make only once, namely the first time, that is if one isn't tempted to have one too many during one's stay in town.

Here one has to add that we were shown to the room by a pretty and very pleasant receptionist, so we avoided the challenge, nor did we succumb to any large excesses during our stay.

The following descriptions have no logical or experiential order, but it makes sense to start with a thought which struck me on the first morning of our stay, that the architect himself most likely uses an electric razor. The miniature washbasin is practically hidden beneath the fixed mixer tap, which makes it totally impossible to get the water up to one's face if one wishes to shave with foam and a safety razor.

Furthermore and while on the subject, the conclusion can obviously also be drawn that the architect only washes his face in the shower, as it is simply impossible to do so if one wishes to use the washbasin.

Sticking to shaving, I definitely draw the conclusion that said architect only uses a cordless electric razor, as there are no electric sockets in this part of the room. I don't dare go as far as to say that the architect most likely has a beard and thus doesn't shave at all, but the possibility does, of course, exist.

In all fairness, it must be said that there was probably an accessible socket near another mirror in the room, there were quite a few of them, so that a normal electric razor with an old-fashioned cord could be used there.

The afore mentioned "washing and freshening up" area with only one washbasin is tiny and not screened off from the double bed. In other words, whatever one does there takes place on an open stage. My wife and I don't have any problems with this and seemingly nor does the architect, which speaks in his favour.

A nightly trip to the toilet, which was situated in the extension of the microscopic washbasin area, is also no joke, if one hasn't brought a torch or doesn't wish to wake one's beloved by turning on the bedside lamp. To turn on the bedside lamp would probably also have been practically impossible without first having activated a series of lights and other devices, as it is virtually impossible to discover which one of the tiny switches belongs to the bedside lamps.

One could, of course, have made a fuss in the reception about all this, but we don't normally do that, unless it's a matter of great importance.

The clever thing about the toilet, which faced the bed, was that it had a glass door on wheels which could be rolled across from the right, while sitting there helplessly facing the bed.

The shower was situated beyond the toilet, which thus formed a sort of entrance to same. A typical "one at a time" arrangement. One could be tempted to believe that the architect didn't realize that all the rooms were meant for two guests.

It can't be as bad as that, however, as all the rooms are equipped with double beds.

On our last night my wife thought of something quite clever as regards a night light, something which we up to then hadn't considered. The hair drier, which only she used and which was fixed to the wall, had a sort of main switch which, when turned on, gave off a little green light. This is probably meant to show its user that it's ready to be used.

Its green glow made it possible to reach the toilet during the night without being in danger of stumbling. Perhaps this was really what the main switch of the hair drier was meant for? There are after all a lot of clever things invented in these days of technology.

To operate the switch panel on the bedside tables would probably in any case require attending a special course, if one were able to read the information at all without a magnifying glass, so we already gave up on that on our first day.

The trial and error method in general led to many exciting and unexpected reactions.

In my younger days I was a passionate bathtub fan. Not so much these days, however, but should I be tempted, it would probably mean a big challenge.

The sarcophagus of a bathtub had a narrow entrance at the opposite end to the mixer tap. First one had to climb up onto the edge of the bathtub and then into same in order to reach and adjust the mixer tap. The sarcophagus itself covered the entire floorspace of the tiny room which was surrounded by glass walls. One had to sit in the tub while it was being filled, if one didn't want to wade in and out as it was happening, in order to operate the mixer tap.

If one is a passionate bathtub user, the water temperature is of the utmost importance. It horrifies me to think of those who would like to have a bath in the tub but who suffer from claustrophobia, they would definitely choose the shower.

The electric blind was silent and nice, but if one doesn't use it, there is an unobstructed view from the neighbour's balcony. It's not that we have a phobia about the neighbour being a peeping tom, but even so.

Most of us have five fingers on each hand. The closet doors, three of them sliding ones, covered the contraption. In addition to having a generous amount of hangers, the contraption also consists of a safe and a mini-bar.

The thing was, however, that the closet doors had to be placed in certain positions in order to gain access to that which one had put in there and wanted to fetch. The operation required great precision and if one wasn't extremely careful, it could easily lead to one's fingers being put in a very awkward position. Luckily we managed to complete our stay with all our fingers intact.

Please don't think that all these minor bagatelles put a negative touch to our stay, but for those of us who belong to the vintage age, small details like those I have given examples of, may represent quite major challenges.

P.S. I apologize for possible mistakes in my descriptions, as the reflection was written from memory.

Turning around - Jan Arnt 2010

The Circle – Renewal

2017

In this context, I don't refer to the Circle which normally is made by means of an instrument. Nor the one drawn by freehand, the one which unintentional presents itself as an oval even if the intention was to make it round. It is the Circle related to renewal I have in mind. Things tend to renew at a certain time. At a closer look this happens when the Circle is closed.

The size of the Circle varies of course, and is dependent of the time between the renewals. The longer time the larger Circle.

Everything need renewal to make continuity possible. In one form or another I believe that most of us have experienced that also cohabitation at times need renewal.

It's like with the flywheel. Supply of power is every now and then required to avoid it stopping.

With experience from business I am convinced that without renewal it comes to a standstill.

Every ting created must, in one form or another be maintained, renewal must be part of all steps to keep the wheels moving.

Goals must be achieved; and circles must be closed while new goals form next circles.

Difficult balance to daily keep the wheels turning while at the same time providing resources to take care of renewal.

Normally a "money bin" to take from does not exist, everything must be created. However, should a "money bin" exist, then undoubtedly it must have been created, and consequently that circle must have been closed.

If the "money bin" has been drained, renewal is needed, understood that it must be filled again as not to be emptied.

In my view much to many people don't understand this, but act as if there is a "money bin" available at any time, as if it existed a Sareptas jar.

Another story is, that what's created in the society unfortunately is made by much too few.

I have been led to know that less than five percent of humanity in this context are creators.

No misunderstanding or discrimination, the creators will always need resources and power to implement their creations, and I believe that is what is needed to create a modern democratic society with acceptable standard of living for everyone.

One will probably never agree the correct balance, but I believe it is socially important that the creators are not discouraged in their performance.

If you are part of curbing the creators, you kill your own future.

Man, is most probably the worst enemy of the man, and in the complex world we live in it is impossible to find the perfect balance between those with and those without the means of creativity.

Many is surely of the opinion that they are creators, even if they are not. Nothing wrong as long their attitude is part of keeping their self-esteem going. However, it may be difficult for them to face the disappointment when lack of success occurs, and they don't understand why.

Making the society more transparent is one of the most important ingredients in creating understanding and respect between humans, at the same time as everything must be done to make the machinery of society straightforwardly for those of us which for different reasons don't use the most important part of our life to understand the complex representing today's society track of content.

In this area I feel that one goes in the wrong direction.

In the effort of creating more workplaces, it seems to me as if many political parties, rather is trying to fill up the public sector, then to look for more cost reducing ways to solve the challenges.

Logically everything must be done to create new meaningful workplaces, but one must put all efforts avoiding to create artificial and not productive ones.

There exists no "money bin", and if taxes are raised above the pain threshold to cover costs for no productive workplaces, it can easily lead to stop of the machinery.

The Circle closes and renewal is a must for continuity.

Without throwing myself into a polemic, I believe we have reached the borderland regarding acceptance of autocracy in the society. The official sector has become so complicated and baffling for us ordinary people that we long ago have given up understanding.

We see to many grey areas.

Furthermore, many of us, myself included, not being interested in prioritising valuable time being spent on understanding the complex.

In private businesses, the mentioned challenges are generally solved by them self, because if not, the business will stop.

Unproductivity is easier disclosed in private businesses and corrective actions happens continuously so that business can continue.

Renewal must be part of the daily life if the wheels shall keep on rolling, something I believe most of us want to happen?

I hope most of us agree that a lot of so called no productive workplaces seen from an economical angel, is both necessary and has its justification but everywhere there are possibilities for rationalisation.

The Circle must close and renewal take place.

King's mouthpiece - Jan Arnt 2010

The Eucalyptus tree

2017

A stormy day on the little parking place belonging to Cortijo Grande Golf club.

It's situated a few kilometre below where I lived in Cabrera while on one of my many visits. For various reasons the course, which originally had 18 holes, had been reduced to 9, something which happened before 1983, being the first time I visited the area.

The only reason I found my way to this part of Spain was due to my father. He was a permanent resident of Jersey Channel Island, but spent the colder part of the year in Alicante in Spain with his family.

In the beginning of the eighties I visited him there, and that's when he told me about Mojacar and Cortijo Grande Golf Course.

That as an answer to my question about his knowledge of the coast from Alicante down to Malaga.

At that time I already had in my mind to look for a place to spend my latter days as a pensioner.

With experience from my school-days in Italy, and from later visits, I had concluded that one had to be far South in that country to benefit from summer temperatures in the winter period.

Although I love Italy, the Southern part was to isolated I thought.

Even in Spain my feeling was that you had to go South to find the place where the sun spends the winter.

My father told me that he I 1976 had been present during the inauguration of Cortijo Grande Golf Course in the Mojacar area. It was a visit he could never forget and told about the fantastic surroundings in the special valley, and the breath-taking nature. At the time he was there he was told that the area had a special micro-climate, with plenty of sun.

At a later date I made a trip with my, at that time cohabitant.

We drove by car down the coast from Alicante, investigated many places along the coast and arrived in Mojacar. Wee lodged at the Parador Hotel down at the coast, and in due time found our way the fifteen kilometre inland to the valley and the golf course.

This trip took place in 1983, seven years after my father had been there, and it was clear to see that the place had seen better days, but the surroundings were spectacular.

Up in the mountain behind the valley we could see what resembled an old fortification. Curiosity took part in us, and after some kilometre driving on a curved but tarmacked road, we reached an urbanisation called Cabrera.

It consisted of a modest centre of town houses and a newly built fortification in old style with tree towers.

In front of the fortification tree greens for lawn bowling had their place. We had never heard of lawn bowling at that time, but we got to know that it was a well-established sport in England.

Apart from the centre town-houses and the fortification, only a few standalone villas could be seen, all in a kind of Moroccan style and painted in a characteristic terracotta colour.

Long story short, that was the first time I met the promoter and the architect Peter Grosschurth. He had taken the challenge of establishing an urbanisation, something very much out of the ordinary. Respect and understanding from the very first moment, and Cabrera became the place where I, many years later, started my active time as a pensioner.

Every time I visited the place after the first, the contact with Peter developed, and I got more and more insight in his dream to create an "Active Retirement Village".

Peter was more than fifteen years older than me and had some fascinating views about further developing the place.

He and his wife had restored an old Cortijo with a goat stable in Cortijo Grande where they lived. What I discovered during my first visit in Cortijo Grande was the impressive allè of eucalyptus trees in a length of a couple of hundred metres on one side of the road. It followed past the old building with the clubhouse, restaurant and parking place.

Someone must some time long ago have planted them, as it is fare in between when you see them in this area.

Giving it a second thought, it's after all not to uncommon in Spain to make use of the eucalyptus trees in the same way we do it with the chess-nut trees in Bygdø Allè in Oslo.

It's about 700 species in this plant family which goes back about 35 to 50 million years. Thereby it is relatively young I understand.

The highest eucalyptus tree is measured to 99,6 metres, which is quite fantastic. The ones I refer to I believe to only be close to thirty.

On the day in question I had, in stormy wind, left my car on the parking place in Cortjo Grande Golf Club.

These days I would never have plaid golf on a day like this, but in those days, time was scares, as it was important to cover the lot.

The beer after the round we enjoyed leeward the restaurant.

Admittedly, the strong wind had created many special situations on the golf course but, as that is equal to everyone everything is OK.

As we arrived from different places, we each went to our car after having said goodbye and thanking each other for an interesting day.

As I approach my little rent a car, I saw the back door and its window totally smashed in, covered by a big branch a couple of meters long and with a diameter of about fifteen centimetre, still covering most of the rear part of the car.

The closest eucalyptus tree is ten fifteen meters from the car, but I could clearly see where the branch had arrived from high up, to be taken by the wind before reaching my car.

I was pleased it had happened while no one was nearby and could have been hit.

This episode took place at the end of the eighties, some 30 years ago, and a lot has happened since then. The golf course unfortunately not playable any longer, but the nature is just as beautiful and the place have kept the micro-climate.

Peter Grosscurth died in 1993 and I married his Swiss widow Marianne in 1998. We lived our first ten years as married in Cabrera, where after, about ten years ago we made it to more flatter land in the same area to make life a little easier in our "Vintage age".

Watches for sale - Jan Arnt 2010

The Mantle piece

2016

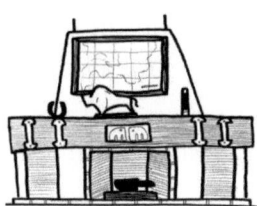

How should anyone be able to imagine that a part of the trunk of a birch tree from a neighbouring garden in Oslo, Norway, should end up as a mantel piece on a fireplace in the South of Spain?

This story is not at all exiting, but I believe it to be quite unusual.

It all started in the late eighties.

After driving from home an ice-cold morning in February, this happens from my home in Gråkamveien in Oslo, Norway,

I observe two men on their way to cut down a few big birch trees in the neighbour's garden.

My immediate thought is that they prepare for dividing the plot into several smaller ones. In those day's plots in this area were relatively big.

On my way to the office I continued dwelling about the birch trees and the reason they had to come down.

Maybe it was so simple as to get more evening sun?

Earlier we had talked about confronting our neighbour on the other side about the possibility to cut a big birch in his garden, which took most of our evening sun.

Nothing brings you closer to a quarrel with your neighbour then these type of situations, so until now it's remained a thought.

Architect Peter Grosscurth in Cabrera in The South of Spain had at this point in time drawn the first sketches of a house I planned to build in his Urbanisation.

Everything was still in the planning phase, but I already had plans with the workroom-office. It should be equipped with a fireplace, and it was not to be the only one in the house. Not only for the cosiness, but at four hundred metres level, the evenings in January and February could easily become chilly.

All houses Peter, until this project had built in his urbanisation, were equipped with fire places, mostly with Moorish motives, and all with cemented Mantle pieces.

The best fire wood used in Spain, matching the Norwegian birch, is olive.

It burns slowly, give good heat and smell, and a cosy atmosphere.

Well in the office, daily challenges took control.

On my way home, I again passed the neighbours garden, and got to see tree big trees, all cut in two lengths, placed beside each other in the snow. They were cleaned for branches, already disposed of, and obviously ready to be cut in suitable lengths and split, to be used as fire wood.

The two having done the job were on their way out the gate, and at that moment the idea struck me that here was my chance.

I stopped the car, got out and confronted the two.

Yes, their idea was to cut the tree trunks in suitable lengths and prepare them for fire wood, although so far no arrangement for sale had been made.

The owner of the property, our neighbour, was an elderly widower. They told that he was uninterested in the wood, making it their job to take care of it all.

I asked if it was possible to buy a few metres of the thickest part of the biggest trunk, and the answer was yes.

To prepare the trunks for firework, they both had to cut and split it, so if someone wanted a large piece that was fine.

I suggested a few hundred kroner, an offer they immediately accepted.

At that time, I drove a big Chevrolet Station car on green targets.

Next morning I arrived prepared with a solid rope at agreed time. Quite some snow had fallen during the night, and the snowplough had not yet reached our addresses.

During wintertime I always kept a set of "knipetak" in my car, and had already put them on the back wheels. (Knipetak is a snap on substitute chain for emergencies).

The car being rather new, was also equipped with a towing hitch, so my plan was ready.

The tree to four metre long trunk, probably weighing a few hundred kilos, I planned to pull after the car from the neighbours garden onto the local road. Then about 150 metres along that one, down our driveway and up to the carport, a distance of another 100 metres.

My part of the trunk they had already cut off, pulled on the snow and

116

placed onto the neighbour's driveway, not far from the gate.

The rope I fastened around one end of the trunk, while the other to the towing hitch on my car. To be able to manoeuvre around three 90-degree bends, it was important with as short as possible distance between the trunk and the car.

The Chevrolet had plenty of horsepower, and with the "knipetak" on, the transport went according to plan.

My partner of course, wondered what this big birch trunk should be used for, as I had not told her about my plan. How she reacted when I told her I don't remember, but she normally was quite sporty when it came to improvisations, so no problems.

I have not yet told that I most probably would have ended up as a carpenter, had it not been for my technical curiosity, and that I as a result of that was sent to Olivetti's technical and commercial school in Italy at an age of seventeen, for later to start in my Stepfather's Office Machine Business, as a technical instructor.

The pleasure of working with wood I have always had.

The birch trunk was kept in the carport at least a couple of years before I thought it dry enough to avoid later "cracks".

When I built the house at Gråkammen with my wife in those days, around 1970, we made a weaving-room for her in conjunction with the launch. She was artistic and possessed talent both for weaving and painting. The room which separated from the launch by a sliding door I, for the occasion turned into a carpeting workshop.

After consulting the Architect Peter Grosscurth in Cabrera, we agreed that the Mantle piece above the fireplace in the office should have a width of 208 centimetres. He would, as long as the measurement was correct, get it installed in due time.

How to get this heavy piece of wood to Spain I had not seriously considered.

Didn't I mention that I drove a big Chevrolet Station car, and didn't that make an opportunity?

Anyhow, the challenge of transport would be taken when time arrived

Before the trunk was moved into the "workshop" for further preparation, the agreed length was cut, and the round trunk became square by means of a chainsaw. Placed on two wooden trestles in the correct height, it was only a matter of attacking it with more suitable tools.

After having finished the Mantle piece, it's exact measurement became 208cm long, 29 cm high and 18 cm in with.

In my book "70 years in communication, about the Max Manus companies", amongst others I also touched the company's engagement in Cabrera, with a pilot project for communication and alarm system.

In connection with that, a lot of equipment was to be transported from Norway.

The largest van was filled with all kind of equipment in conjunction with the project – and the home made Mantle piece.

Two guys made turn at the wheel and made it through many exiting experiences on the various borders, safely to Cabrera with everything included.

The transformed Norwegian birch trunk became the Mantle piece in the new house in 1990, and still has it'd dominant place there, completely free of any cracks or other defects.

King bird with knee pants

The Scarecrow

September 2017

It's a fact that where we live in the South of Spain, along the thirteenth hole on a golf course, a variety of birds also seem to have understood that it's wonderful to live.

As our flat is on the first floor with an uninhibited flat under us, at the end of a block of four, plenty of Sparrows, Swallows in the season, and Pigeons, fight between themselves to also make a living.

Our cleaning lady, coming once a week, spend half her time making the terrace presentable, as our winged friends seem to compete about who can make the most droppings exactly there.

At times it seems like they are also joined by competitors from other districts.

Apart from the inconvenience, we love to have the birds around, although we at times get swallows into the living room. Once we had three at the same time, having a great struggle to get them safely out again.

Another downside is that they build their nests all over the place, but obviously one can not only have the pleasure.

While on our yearly trip to Oslo during the month of August this year, my wife registered how quiet it was in the flat. Apart from the sound normally coming from a city, the only birds we hear now and then are the Seagulls.

We don't miss the heat in Spain, it being the main reason for us going here, but the sound of the birds we look forward to return to.

Well, just the sound of the birds and seeing them is lovely, but not so much what goes with them apart from that.

One day we walked around in the district, it was a slight breeze in the air, my wife discovered something strange on the top of a building. Could it be a "big bird of prey" of a kind? Its big wings were spread above the roof top.

At the first glance, I saw it was one of those Scarecrows looking like a big bird. A black bird-like kite, fastened to the top of what looked like a fishing-rod by means of a thin line. It moved from side to side and up and down according to the winds variation in strength.

I have not seen many of this type before, but the next couple of days, more aware of their existence, we saw a few more.

My wife got very excited and insisted we had to find out where they could be bought so we could bring a couple back to Spain.

I told her the idea was good, but as we normally have little wind in the area, it wouldn't serve the purpose. As well I told her that with the size they seemed to have it wouldn't fit in our suitcases.

My wife is Swiss and can be quite stubborn, so when she again, not paying much notice to my arguments, claimed we could surely get a smaller size that could fit, I surrendered and saw no other way out but to try to get hold of them.

On the first floor of the block of apartments we live in, there is an office for care-taking and security. I passed by and asked if they had any idea of where I could get hold of the Scarecrows, the type I had seen on top of some of the buildings in the surrounding. Immediately they had no answer, but would be happy to investigate and send me a mail.

So far perfect, and only minutes later entering the flat, I heard a "signal" in my iPhone. Printing out the content on my PC, which of course got the mail at the same time, I had two addresses in my hand. One being a chain called "Biltema" – (Car Theme), and the other "skadedyrsikring" – (Pest protection).

As we have no car while in Norway, very little knowledge about public transport and that taxies being extremely expensive, I figured that this was one of the times I would make use of the office of the family business. I still have very good contact with one of the old timers from my active days.

The same moment I hit his name on the iPhone, an incoming call took priority and I heard my friend Christian's voice.

Hei George, I have a gap in my golf schedule, and was hoping we could have a coffee and a chat. We had a pending agreement that he would call when that was the case.

You wouldn't believe it, but I was just calling Terje in the office for some help to get me one of these Scarecrow.

I could almost see the question mark in his face through the phone! What?

An hour later he picked me up and I explained the whole story.

The chase was on.

He knew the only "Biltema" shop in Oslo, situated as far on the other side of town as one could get. "Biltema" is otherwise a big chain spread all over the country.

Twenty minutes later we entered the enormous shop and presented our mission. It took a little time before they first found it in their thick colourful catalogue and that they were sold out.

What next, where else could we get them? Apparently, no other shops did sell them, so where could we find the closest "Biltema"?

The answer was: in a town called Drøbak, close to forty kilometres south on the east side of the Oslo fjord. They did check on the computer, and saw they had a few in stock.

With good spirit and plenty to talk about we headed for Drøbak.

Pleasant reception, but they were unfortunately also sold out. How could that be, we just got the information in Oslo….? – excuses - nothing doing.

On our question, they told us that the closest shop would be in Hamar, a city one hundred and twenty-five kilometres north of Oslo, plus the forty we had already done to the south of the city. A total of more than one hundred and sixty.

As Christian had picked me up at eleven and it was now passed one, it was time for a coffee.

As he knew the district we passed by another mall to look around, resulting in me getting a couple of pullovers.

While having the coffee Christian came to mention that in our Golf Club in Oslo, Bogstad, they had a few of these type of Scarecrows.

Playing golf almost every day in the season, he knows everyone in the club and calls the chief administrator. He could not remember from where they had been bought, but indicated a name.

- Thank you and over and out.

On the road again Christin pulls out his Tom Tom navigator and calls 1881, the Norwegian number information.

The helpful lady on the other end could not find a matching name, but Christian is not the one to give up. What about trying this change in the spelling.....? After a couple of attempts, bingo, she got a match. Thank you and I'll call back if it doesn't work.

I was of course listening in on all this as it happened on the car phone.

No presentation of a company name, just "hallo". Are you the one with the Scarecrows?

He was the one. He had no shop, was the importer and had his stock in the basement of a modern office building just outside Lillestrøm, a little city seventeen kilometres north of Oslo.

Only close to sixty kilometres driving, we had still plenty to chat about, and as we were now totally committed to make the day a success, Christian programmed the address in the Tom Tom and off we went.

I forgot to tell that I, in my excitement of finding my two pullovers, had forgotten my reading glasses in the shop where I bought them while trying them out. As they are tailor made we had to make a turn and try to retrieve them.

First turn on the motorway and back to a smiling lady who had found them.

The last thing Christian had done on the phone was to make an agreement to call the guy when we entered Lillestrøm, to agree where and when to meet him. He was obviously not permanently in the warehouse.

As agreed we called him back, explained our position and made it ten minutes to "rendez-vous".

As we entered the parking place, so did another car.

Are you looking for us, and we looking for you? Perfect timing.

Down in the basement Jan had an unbelievable selection of hunting equipment, and among it all, what we were looking for. They only came in one size, but in two colours, black and brown.

Less than ten minutes later, we headed back towards town with four Scarecrows, two of each colour. They were exactly matching the ones we had seen on the top of the buildings around where we stayed.

Mission accomplished, and even at a good price.

Christian had now built up an appetite for a baguette, so on our way back we made a visit to a golf course we both had played year back in time.

Sitting on the beautiful built in terrace and taking in the lovely view, we could but agree it had been a fine day.

When letting me off a little over five, as usual we agreed that he and his wife would come down to visit us when the golf season had come to an end in Norway and the snow had arrived.

No need to tell that my wife was happy when I showed her the catch of the day, and when she realised that they even entered the suitcases, though with some slight bending.

Now it only remains to see if they will work to satisfaction? – We will see.

Bird in flight - Jan Arnt 2010

The sun-eaters lights us up

2015

How is it possible to make such a heading? First an explanation of what I have in mind using the phrase which for many must be difficult to understand: sun-eater.

I refer to these mysterious contraptions which eats the energy from the sun and change it into energy, yes, what else than energy.

Of course it is incorrect when I say they eat the energy.

The sun is not in any way consumed as we transfer its light to energy.

It is of course not a matter of eating the sun, that is by no way correct.

The sun is by no means drained for anything when we convert its sunbeams into energy.

Today's search to find alternative sources of energy creates competition, which is good.

First a little about the state of art, based on my limited knowledge.

By far the greatest and best built out sources of energy must be oil and cold. These however, have the bad property we all are aware of, namely that they are environmentally unfriendly.

Then we have some more environmentally friendly ones, such as gas, waves, wind, hydroelectric and of course the sun.

When it comes to atom power plants, we know they are extremely efficient, but we need only to be reminded of the last tragedy in Japan to be very careful about spreading to many of them around for reason of security.

We are constantly reminded about how long these various sources of energy will last, seemingly something the experts knows a lot about.

Despite different opinions about the speed of progress related to the extraction of particularly the oil and coal, for environmental reasons, it is obvious that we can't base our self on these sources lasting forever.

There is a great deal of unity about the fact that our globe is not benefiting from the waste products that these energy sources is leaving behind.

As mentioned, there exists a continues disagreement about the volume of extraction of the various energy sources, logically influencing the prices and not unexpectedly leading to much polemic about the subject.

Strong forces are active to stop the extraction, a view fully understandable from those with that perception; after all their aim is to save those of us who don't understand anything.

If it was only so simple.

Some believe slowing the extraction will secure future generations access to these energy sources in a longer period.

Also that argument, seen isolated, one must respect.

Seen with my eyes however, this setting is greatly egocentric, again seen isolated.

A postponement in short term yes but, obviously as I see it, not a protracted reasonable solution. On the contrary, unbelievably irresponsible.

In my younger days, we probably where not fully aware of the environmental disadvantages following the extraction of these energy sources in the same way as today, although the subject was on the table.

Most probable, people involved must have been aware of the disadvantages, not the least because of Norway's heavy engagement in the oil exploration.

I always had my clear point of view on this subject, so what could be done?

By no means nationalisation and state control. Such solutions will never give good solutions. On the contrary,

I believe the solution must be to let the gigantic oil industry, or rather, all industries related to exploration of energy sources creating environmental unfriendly emissions, them self be part of the financing of developing alternative energy sources.

A new form of the Norwegian oil fund in addition to the one we have.

Nothing wrong with the Norwegian oil fund which, when this was put on paper, represented 7000 milliard Norwegian kroner. If we didn't have that, the relative short economical future for Norway would seem bleak.

What then about the alternative solutions for environmentally friendly energy, and the financing needed to find the best solutions?

It should not be difficult to find sensible and for all party's acceptable ways to reach the goal.

There are solutions to the challenge, it's only a matter to get the parties taking on the research.

Who could be the parties in question?

The determinative and coordinating part must by nature be the state in a far-reaching case like this.

The financing part, should amongst others be those companies paying tax because of their profits related to exploration of or another involvement in dealing with today's organic energy sources, those who creates unwanted waste products.

Simply said, a substantial part of the tax money coming from the above mentioned, must be set off.

This sources must then, under strong scrutiny, subsidize those who justifiably have the means to work with and develop alternative environmentally friendly energy sources.

The division of the subsidize of course represents a challenging act of balance, but will be made practical by forming an impartially organ consisting of experts in various fields.

The technical follow up of the various developments can and must take place by another impartially organ consisting of technical experts.

I wish I could believe that a general tax cut for those who today are engaged in the business of extracting environmentally unfriendly energy sources, would lead to sufficient funds being used in developing alternative solutions. Unfortunately, I don't believe it would.

Motivation is the driving force in all progress. Nothing is impossible if the conditions are facilitated.

My personal hope is that one day solutions will be found to tame the solar energy is such way that it can be the dominating contributor to our ever-rising demand for energy.

The sunscreens

August 2017

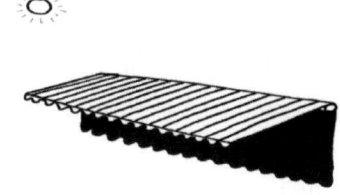

I see no reason to keep my lucky numbers secret. Everyone is free to use them in any situation,

They are 14 and 17. From the moment I became conscious about lucky numbers I chose these two.

As time went by I added 7 and 21.

However, I did stick to the first two, as four was too much to keep in order.

Then, have they been my lucky numbers?

Yes, I mean they have. Although I've never kept any statistics, and it is ages since I bought the last lottery ticket and participated in any form of gambling, I still believe in the numbers fourteen and seventeen.

My wife has no lucky numbers, as she already early in life thought she wasn't a winner in lottery.

What on earth has sunscreens to do with my lucky numbers you may ask?

This is the story:

Where we live in Valle del Este in the South of Spain, we early discovered that the sun, which we have more of than in most places in Spain, already at lunchtime covers the whole terrace, and the longer into the afternoon and early evening, the more of it we get into the living room.

Immediately after we moved in we built what we call a "summer-launch", covering one third of the terrace. It is placed parallel to the main launch, and reduced the terrace in front to 4 x 15 meters

The "summer launch" is constructed by aluminium profiles, with sliding doors in front and partly glass- walls in the back and on the side opposite to the main launch.

The roof is made by milky plastic, as golf-balls every now and then tend to make us a visit.

Soon we experienced that the heat became unbearable if the window and sliding-doors were closed, so very soon we installed a sunscreen under the roof. This became a great help in keeping the sun out, but didn't at all cool down the room.

So far, we have done nothing with this challenge, but realize that the plastic roof must be changed.

The terrace in front of the main launch is equipped with decorative cement beams.

Enabling the garden furniture to be kept there regardless of the weather, we installed a plastic roof above the cement beams, the same type as in the "summer-launch".

Is it something about adapting, that one must first experience before one decides what to do to make life more pleasant?

In the beginning, we acquired to parasols with cemented movable foundations.

To avoid direct sun when we sat on the terrace, these were moved around in line with the sun's invariable migration over the sky, at the same time as changing wind directions had to be taken into consideration to avoid them tilting.

Anyhow, they were not easy to move, particularly as the foundations were heavy and the parasols were placed under the decorative cement beams.

Only one summer-season passed after the roof was put in place, before a retractable sunscreen, the size of the roof, was installed.

This covered half the terrace of 4 x 15 meter and provided shadow into the afternoon and early evening.

As with most sunscreens in our part of the world, they are in front equipped with a decorative "wave".

Sitting under it, independent of it being day evening or night, we have a feeling of intimacy.

As mentioned, it gave us good sun protection through the day and the early afternoon, but from then on until sunset we were strongly exposed.

As our daily activities away from home prevent us from using the terrace during the day, we mainly use it in the afternoon and evenings. We then get the feeling of intimacy but no protection from the sun.

One evening I sat on the terrace philosophising about what next to do to protect us from the late afternoon and evening sun, and as the sunscreen was pulled out I happened to look at its decorative front.

For unknown reasons I started counting the "waves", and regardless doing it from right to left or reversed I came to fourteen.

Surprised and happy I was reminded of my lucky number but didn't dwell more about it.

The obvious and the best solution was a front sunscreen, which in a closed rolled up position could be placed between the two cement pillars on each side in front of the terrace. It could be cracked down to 90 degrees and thereby give shelter from the intense afternoon and evening sun.

It would obviously be about a meter narrower than the roof sunscreen, but including the cement pillars it would do the job perfectly.

With these thoughts in mind I decided to contact the supplier.

After sun set, when closing the window and the sliding-doors in the "summer-launch", I thought about the fourteen "waves" on the terrace sunscreen, and took a closer look at this one.

After counting, again from both sides, I came to seventeen, the same as my other lucky number. Well, there was a difference in with between the terrace sunscreens and this one, but that it ended up with three more "waves"and became seventeen was quite interesting.

Well, after all, both my lucky numbers could be no harm I thought.

Ordering the front screen for the terrace, it turned out that the company had changed owner and name. However, everything went well both with measuring, quote and order, and to our satisfaction they installed the sunscreen two to three weeks later.

We now had the perfect solution and could, with the crank, adjust it according to the suns movement.

Although also this screen had the traditional "wave" decoration, I only at a much later time came to think about it.

Quite right – I counted fourteen "waves".
Two lucky number fourteen and one seventeen. All good things come in trees - better it couldn't be I thought.

As you may have understood, my wife is not particularly interested in these things, so consequently I didn't involve her in these coincidences.

Now, only one third of the terrace was without sunscreen. That part of the terrace is where our outdoor dining-table is situated. If we take of the chair pillows, both the table and the chairs will resist the rear rain we get.

Inside we have a dining-table seating four, but as we seldom have guests we hadn't until this time prioritized any sunscreen on this terrace.

Having been accustomed to the intimacy having a sunscreen roof over our head, we ultimately decided to put one up also on this last part of the terrace. As it's not a sitting area and eventual dinners anyhow would take place after sunset, there was no reason to protect it from the afternoon sun.

New contact with the supplier, which again delivered at right terms and time. Admittedly, he didn't match the grey tone perfectly, but then, one can't expect every ting to go according to plan.

This screen definitively makes the terrace complete, fulfilling all our needs.

Even if this screen in no way have the same measurement as the others, I probably don't need to mention that also this had the decorating "waves" in front, and guess how many? Seventeen of course.

Two times fourteen and two times seventeen "waves" on four sunscreens, all installed at different times over a few years by two different suppliers.

Now it's only remains to see if this gives a countdown?

.

The Train Accident at Pålsboda

September 2012

Pålsboda is a tiny place not far from Ørebro in Sweden and Ørebro is situated to the north west of the lakes Venneren and Vetteren in the southern part of the country. More accurately put, in the municipality of Hallsberg in Ørebro county in the province of Nærke.

The number of registered inhabitants in 2005 was 1,524.

This is probably for non-Swedes like having to orient themselves in the books written by Stig Larsson, Henning Mankell and Jonas Jonasson, when it comes to geography.

But then Sweden is to the Swedes the navel of the world. I hasten to add that this is probably true of most countries, that their citizens see their own country as the navel of the world.

I have never been back there since this episode took place sometime around 1950. I can't be more precise, as these are only memories which I'm trying to bring back to life more than sixty years later.

The incident is also not registered in Wikipedia, but they admit that their registration of train accidents is far from complete.

Enough said, for a boy at the age of about 11, alone on the night train from Stockholm to Oslo, it was a powerful experience.

I had been to visit my father and his new wife in Stockholm for the first time, with all the great experiences that entailed. The post war rationing in Norway meant everything was especially appreciated during this visit, which culminated in me being accompanied to the night train to Oslo and one of the first sleeping compartments in carriage number 3.

As it was late in the evening, I went straight to bed as the train chugged out of the central train station in Stockholm. And chug the train did as it was being pulled by a steam engine which was common in those days.

All the impressions from the visit made me fall asleep immediately and dream of visits to the Grøna Lund amusement park and zoo as well as of bubblegum, chocolate and a lot more.

Someone knocks loudly at the compartment door, trying to open it. This proves not to be too easy but, after some time and a lot of loud-voiced talk, the conductor managed to open the door and ascertain with relief that I as the only passenger in the compartment was unhurt. I had during the resulting chaos sat up in bed and turned on the light.

Unhurt from what? There I was, awakened from my deep sleep by people who seemed ever so excited in the middle of the night.

I was informed that there had been an accident and that I had to get dressed, grab my suitcase and get out.

I pull up the blinds to have a look and get my first shock. Just a few meters away there's a derailed car, missing its side wall and letting me get a glimpse, as far as I can recall, of the interior of all the compartments in about half its length. That it had been derailed I understood as the entire carriage sloped down towards the left, in other words in the direction we were going.

I managed to get myself organized, put the few things I'd taken out back in the suitcase and left the compartment. In the corridor I didn't see anyone else, but through the window, across a couple of tracks, I noticed a station building bearing the name "PÅLSBODA".

If my memory serves me right, everything sloped down as I walked towards the exit. I believe the first set of wheels on carriage number 3, which was the one I was in, had been derailed. The engine had, after it had been derailed, continued straight through the building and left a hole which looked like the opening of a tunnel.

Standing in a daze on the platform, I was taken by helpful people to the waiting room which was completely untouched and intact. Together with several others, who probably had enough with themselves and their problems, I was left sitting there alone waiting for what would happen.

I can't remember anyone talking to me until we some time later were told that we would be picked up in buses and taken to Oslo.

In the meantime we had registered sirens from both ambulances fire engines and police cars. Furthermore, there must have been crews of helpers come to investigate the amount of damage.

Those who were supposed to pick me up at Vestbanestasjonen , the train station in Oslo's West End, must have had quite a shock when they got there, being told there had been an accident and heard that the passengers were expected by bus several hours later.

What they weren't told was how many were injured and if there were any casualties.

In other words quite dramatic.

I don't remember anything from the bus journey, or meeting my family upon arrival.

What has struck me later in life when I've read about or watched on TV, reports of accidents of various kinds, is how psychologist are brought in to help alleviate the trauma of those involved. In those days that invention hadn't been made I suppose.

How one can sleep through an event like this is totally incomprehensible and let it be said, I don't think the experience left me with any scars, in one way or another.

It might be that the above doesn't quite match reality but seen in retrospect, it is as I perceived it as an eleven-year-old at the time. I believe the train driver was killed and around 35 people had to go to hospital.

After having read the above last night, I was lying in bed going through the memories I have of the event one more time. Not that it means anything in the context, but it's quite possible that I was in carriage number 4 and that it was three carriages in front of this one which derailed and that my carriage actually remained standing on the track. Well, it immediately strikes me that next summer, when we're staying in Oslo any way; it would be interesting to drive over to Pålsboda to check what details exist about what happened as well as the exact date and year of the accident. No one I know would be able to give me this information.

I must have kept thinking about it and it suddenly occurred to me that I mentioned something about it in my Ego Presentation at my Rotary Club many years ago and believe it or not, today I found a copy of my presentation from 1987. The following is a direct transcript from the presentation and probably the more correct version.

"My father whom I last saw just before we left Sweden, I met again at the age of 11. I took the train on my own to Stockholm. He was still convalescent, had epilepsy as a result of his injuries from the bombing of Åndalsnes, but had just got married again to a Swedish woman.

What does one remember from this meeting, well, the return train journey was very special? A derailment of dimensions at, was it Pålsboda in Sweden? 30 or 40 people ended up in hospital and at least one person was killed if I remember correctly. I was awakened by the conductor who couldn't open the door of my compartment.

My carriage which was number 4 had been derailed, while the carriages ahead of mine were lying about helter-skelter".

That should be a more correct version without it making any difference to the context.

I have fortunately not had any similar experiences since then.

What happens? - Jan Arnt 2010

The Waiting Room

October 2014

Or, perhaps better put, the waiting rooms. My experience so far in life is that it often ends up being several waiting rooms throughout a lifetime with an increasing number of visits as one reaches one's "vintage" age.

How many times in one's life has one sat in a waiting room? As one first made one's acquaintance with these "places of waiting", and that must be why they are called waiting rooms, one was probably safely ensconced on mother's lap. Nobody goes clear, it's only the reason for one's visits that varies.

Everyone has specific memories from their visits to the waiting room and the results of these visits vary, of course, from being positive to affecting one's further existence. The results of the visits are in themselves timeless. Everything happens or doesn't happen regardless of time.

Today we're sitting there, once again, my wife and I. This time at the "Virgen del Mar" hospital in Almeria in the South of Spain. It's my wife's turn this time, she's about to have a "gastroscopia". We don't know how long it will take but everything will be done under anaesthesia, which is good.

This doesn't have anything to do with the waiting room in itself but we are, at least, sitting there at the moment. We have arrived with time to spare, almost an hour early. We have gradually come to know this hospital very well and they have given us the best possible treatment throughout the years. According to our private medical insurance, this is where we have to come for our minor or major ailments of which there have, of course, been a few over the years; we do, after all, belong to the "vintage" age.

In the reception we already met a married couple, the husband English and the wife Spanish, whom my wife knows well from before. Later on, the wife of another married couple, whom we have also known for many years, came along and could tell us that her husband had been staying at the hospital for days and was being examined for a possible operation.

I would like to meet the person who hasn't got his or her thoughts racing upon entering a hospital.

Approximately ten people are gathered here in this particular waiting room, and as some get summoned to their various consultations, new ones appear. This time we are, as far as we can see, the only foreigners, but even if this might set us apart, we all have something in common, everyone being equipped with the big white envelope containing their referrals. This we were given in the reception before being told which waiting room, or "sala de espera" as it's called in Spanish, we had to go to.

A relatively young woman with spasms, completely confined to a motorized wheelchair, is sitting there with her father, as are a couple of heavily pregnant young women, both in excellent spirits and full of expectation. One of them accompanied by a woman friend and the other with her partner. A middle-aged woman, elegantly dressed, her mobile permanently against her ear but unlike most other Spaniards, speaking softly. It turned out later that she was waiting for her daughter, who after a while came out smiling from her consultation. She had obviously not "won the lottery". Another middle-aged woman, also elegantly dressed, suddenly gets up to run an errand seemingly without purpose. Her handbag remains on her chair until she gets back, this is obviously not a place where one expects such things to be snatched.

Nor on this occasion are we to be spared the appearance of a man, they seem to be everywhere, communicating on his mobile in a loud voice, while walking back and forth in the relatively modest in size, and otherwise relatively quiet, waiting room. The reason for it being relatively quiet is that there are no children present, apart from those of the pregnant women, but they are seemingly quiet compared to the rest of us.

For those fluent in Spanish it's impossible to avoid capturing the entire content of the various conversations taking place, but here it's all done in a polished Andalusian dialect, incomprehensible to those with only Castilian school Spanish. Nor am I the right person to comment in detail about this, as my own Spanish only consists of a limited number of monosyllabic words.

What one also notices is that almost none of the patients are alone, thus the conversations. One or more family members or friends are always ready to come along if someone has to pay a visit to the waiting room and in most cases they also sit in on the consultations themselves.

A doctor appears in a doorway on the other side of the corridor, which separates the waiting room from the territory of the doctors.

He turns around in the corridor, calls out a name and is given an instant response from a new patient. As the doctor opens the door again to enter with his new patient, a few meters inside the door I glimpse a bed, which I can only see from the foot end. The green duvet covers everything except my wife's head, which I immediately recognize from the hair, as I can't see her face. She's obviously sleeping off the "high" after her treatment, which up to now has lasted about three quarters of an hour. The envelope containing the papers, which she had taken with her as she left her handbag and jacket for me to look after and which it had taken close to ten minutes to organize at the counter in the reception, lay on top of the duvet like "stamp" showing that she had been through the process.

Hers was the only bed I could see during the few seconds the door was open and I returned to my thoughts. Shortly after she was called in, I had put down the book I had brought in order to keep my thoughts at bay. Keeping one's thoughts at bay ought to be a subject all its own in today's world of unlimited access to information, both that which is good and useful and that which we could easily do without. So, why don't we just pick up that which is good and useful?

Thoughts, what else would be tumbling around in one's head whilst one is sitting there in the waiting room? Thoughts about all the others who are sitting there as well as those one has about one's own reason for being there, whether it has to do with oneself or, as in this case, with my wife.

It's difficult to speak about the way others feel, but I myself have a very vivid imagination which I at times struggle to keep under control.

It is often the worst scenarios which come to the forefront and which one has to fight to get under control. After all, not everyone draws one's last breath from stomach cramps.

Another fifteen minutes go by before the door on the other side of the corridor opens once again and my wife appears in the doorway.

The results of the day's exploration, she'd receive in about ten days, after which another visit to the waiting room with its accompanying thoughts would surely be called for; and so it was.

As usual we're there with time to spare and sit watching people coming and going. A middle-aged woman, obviously Spanish, sits down next to my wife on the other side, after having greeted us with a smile. After a couple of minutes she, as most do after having sat down, pulls out her mobile phone. We see her marking a number but immediately notice that she doesn't put the phone to her ear but holds it up so that she's facing the screen, making me think she's about to Skype. Sure enough, but not the way it's normally done in a video conversation. She holds the mobile in front of her in her left hand, smiling and gesticulating at the screen as she at great speed communicates with her right hand in sign language. No sound is heard from her or the other person, so it's obvious that he or she is also deaf mute. After a while she disconnects, puts her mobile back in her handbag and smiles happily at us.

Fantastic, we suddenly realize what a remarkable aid modern technology can be, especially when used as in this case.

Neither of us had seen or thought of it in this light before, but the episode made us think more deeply about all those whose lives have been given new meaning this way.

Things Take Time

January 2015

That things take time is a very apt expression. We all experience both the positive and negative aspects of our bureaucracy as we throughout life get more and more acquainted with it. I don't in any way believe that the Spanish bureaucracy is better or worse than the Norwegian one, but I'm looking forward with anticipation to seeing what will happen to my personal taxes.

Since I, after retiring, gave up my Norwegian residency, back in 2006, it has been made clear to me that I have to pay my taxes in Spain and not in Norway.

Immediately after retiring I called NAV (the Norwegian Labour and Welfare Services) to find out what to do about taxes after moving my permanent residency to Spain.

No sooner had I asked my question before the female functionary in a brusque voice said something like: "Don't think it's that simple to avoid taxes".

To make a long story short, feeling powerless myself, I let the powers that be "win", hung up the phone and have since then paid my taxes in Norway.

In other words, greeted the way I was, I gave up at the very beginning.

Everything has gone smoothly and about 33% of my pension has remained in Norway despite my having stayed there on average less than a month a year since that time.

Likewise, have I been excluded from the Norwegian welfare annals. This despite my seemingly reasonable contribution to the Norwegian authorities.

Up to now I have paid several tens of thousands to Norwegian and Spanish lawyers and the case is running its course. As in most matters, everything will work out, but that things take time is certain. Now, at the end of June, I was able to pay my Spanish tax, without being given a penalty, retroactively for five years. It's good to have a family who is able to provide support. The process has now started to get the Norwegian taxes for the last five years refunded and how long that will take and what it will cost, only time will show.

My Norwegian driving licence which I've had, without any black marks against it, since I was eighteen, I wasn't able to renew in Norway last time I tried.

Fair enough, it would have to be exchanged for a Spanish one. No problem, such matters are dealt with by a so-called "Gestoria". It ended up taking nearly five months, so yes, things take time.

I must add that after having handed in my Norwegian licence at the start of the process, I was, after about two months, given a document allowing me to drive, while my Spanish driving permit was being prepared. In other words, things happen, but that they take time is certain.

What actually got me triggered about things taking time had nothing to do with the above.

Far more serious things happen around the world and the tragic event which took place at Charlie Hebdo in Paris on January ninth, immediately makes me think about the issue involving human integration. This subject is, of course, very complex and I'm by no means sufficiently competent to debate it, but one has naturally enough made one's reflections on the matter.

Race, religion and culture. The development has been far to quick in my opinion.

Integration or so-called adaptation is impossible, at least over a short period of time. One has to let things take their time when worldwide religions and cultures of various kinds are to be welded together. Another matter is why one, come hell or high water, has to force the coming about of this integration?

When it comes to human integration, one has to take a look at what happens in the animal world, if not, it will go terribly wrong; things take time.

It seems, however, that we are stupid enough to believe that it is possible to achieve without giving it sufficient time. Time is an ingredient we evidently don't have enough of.

I, who am totally against trying to stop or delay development in general, have to say that when it comes to human integration, it can't take place at the same pace as other forms of development.

Seen with my eyes, there are endless examples these days showing us that we are on the wrong track and it's difficult to believe that it can become anything but worse.

Tolerance is important, but when the differences are as great as they seem to be at the moment, even though most of us in the western world are of the opinion that we are talking about minorities, we have to admit that we are talking about diametrical opposites as regards culture and ideology. It has to be taken far more seriously, than to believe that everything will be well, if only we let a natural integration take place.

Show me one place, remaining within Europe, where we have a single example of a really successful human integration, which has taken place over a short period of time.

Examples might possibly be given, but I don't believe there are many.

Segregation, I don't like the word ghetto, is becoming more and more common. The so-called integration, the way we perceive it to be, isn't happening. Is it against nature? I'm again referring to the animal world.

Gradually one learns to live with a sort of respect for one another, which in itself is a good thing, of course, but herein lies the challenge.

Extremists have always existed, in all cultures, and they will always continue to exist. Groups with radical views likewise.

They blossom in light of changing economic and charitable development . Many of the so-called "new citizens" don't understand or won't accept, naturally enough, that not everything is served on a silver platter, since that is what they have risked life and limb to reach our part of the world for. Things take time.

England, with its two and a half million Muslims, is said to be faced with an additional challenge. They have, as we know, enough immigrants from before, both legal ones from other EU countries and those from other parts of the world. A large number of Sharia marriages are taking place. It is said that more than one hundred thousand Sharia marriages among people under thirty have been arranged and that the number is increasing. This happens in order to avoid responsibility according to British law, as women in such marriages have no rights under British law. These marriages are not officially registered and often include polygamy.

Against those who "loudly and clearly" express that we are the enemy and must be wiped out, there is only one answer, in my opinion, and one which must be expressed "loudly and clearly".

No mercy.

It can't possibly be right to wait until they might be ready to change their minds, can it?

Things take time.

Ready to fly - Jan Arnt 2010

Tolerance and Compromise

2017

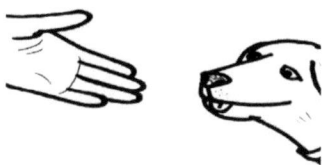

First very plain about the word tolerance. It means to withstand and hold out, not physical strength. "Tolerance is the ability to withstand living with those who have different opinions and attitudes and who then acts, in other words those which you do not usually accept".

This should be a reflection for all of us.

Most of us will add something more direct to being tolerant, something more straight to the point. Either you tolerate this or that or you don't.

Seen from that angle we clearly speak of something black or white or what? That is not the case.

The description of tolerance state that we talk about a balancing Act.

One tolerate to a greater or lesser extent which is good after my opinion.

In other words, I claim for a fact that tolerance is not black or white.

Tolerance is an Act of balance and Compromise is the weight on the weight making it balancing.

Compromise must be part of balancing.

It is impossible to make an Act of balance without adding the ingredient of give and take- Compromise, and that I think is good.

Imagine how well they are feeling, the ones that mean they are tolerant. Such an attitude becomes subjective, as others undoubtedly may have a divergent view.

Standing a litter further away, a little more on the outside, pretending to have a more objective view, may give one an easier opportunity to make a statement about the one in questions ability to appear tolerant.

The complex that tolerance represent I have no prerequisite to throw me deeper into and will not do so, as it is a factor in all people's lives.

How we as individuals relate to tolerance is of the greatest importance for our identity.

As I have made Compromise part of the heading, and claim it as a condition for tolerance to be practised, I will dwell a little with this word.

One explanation goes as follows: "A Compromise is a result of actions where no one of the parties gets its will 100%, but everyone gets something".

Compromise, maybe one of the most important words, looking apart from love.

Even when using the phrase "unconditional love", at time there is a need for a little Compromise?

Putting your hand forward to your enemy is according to me not the same as to turn the other cheek on. In principal I am totally for the one with the cheek but life experience has thought me that this approach seldom results in success. The reason being that man is the worst enemy of man.

On the other hand, to stretch out a hand as a start, particularly when it is done with good will, does not result in an either-or situation, meaning that either one gets a slap when the other cheek is turned towards one, or one does not.

As far as I know the Bible does not speak about a loving pat on the cheek or does it?

Maybe I have reached this conclusion after having most of my life, before I became a pensioner, had dogs.

From I was only six my best friend was our English Setter Pet.

Having to do with dogs one knows that the best way to approach a stranger dog, is to carefully stretch out your hand. One will quickly experience if this invitation to closer contact is successful.

Luckily I have still both hands with full sets of fingers, and have only the best experience with this approach.

I will not dwell further with this comparison, everyone has their own experience, but what I try to emphasize is that the situation is not black or white.

Unfortunately, we human have a sad tendency to make thing black or white. Everything become more easy making thing black or white, but also thus more incorrect.

A Balanced Tolerance with the aid of Compromise is necessary. Give a little and take a little, none of the parties feel they are with their back against the wall.

To simplify everything is not always the best solution, understood as looking at the situation as black or white. Because of such simplifications, often unnecessary discontent occurs, resulting in that Tolerance with the aid of Compromise is put on a big test.

Tolerance is an ingredient in a variety of situations, without me dwelling to much about it.

The total lack of tolerance related to acceptance of different religions is probably what has caused the biggest challenges on our planet throughout the times.

Maybe not so strange as this is where we find the most fanatics, clearly examples of people with black or white opinions.

Bird on the head - Jan Arnt 2010

Traffic lights

Feb. 2016

This introduction I've taken from Wikipedia to bring some light about the development of them.

The world's first, manually operated gas-lit traffic signal was short lived. Installed in London December 1868, it exploded less than a month later, injuring or killing its policeman operator. Traffic control started to seem necessary in the late 1890s and Earnest Sirrine from Chicago patented the first automated traffic control system in 1910. It used the words "STOP" and "PROCEED", although neither word lit up

Traffic lights alternate the right of way to users by displaying lights of a standard colour (red, amber (yellow), and green) following a universal colour code the typical sequence of colour phases:

When I reinvented the wheel, it wasn't of course a matter of inventing the round wheel once more. The aim was making it turn by itself by means of an "off the shelve" electric motor. Not an electric HUB motor. That was invented in 1884 by Wellington Adams.

Talking about reinventing the traffic light, it's not a matter of changing the basic red, green and yellow light, as they, after all this years, are well accepted.

Now, it's a matter of making the existing traffic lights safer for motorists and pedestrians, even three times as safe.

How often don't we hear about accidents happening because the ones involved didn't catch the attention of the traffic light.

A prerequisite is that the lights are working with "LED", light- emitting diodes, and three light fixtures which each individually can present red, green and yellow. They already exist.

Let's start with all three being green. If yellow transition to red is a wish, one of the three turns to yellow, while the other two remains green, or if preferred, two turns yellow and one green.

When this sequence is over, all three lamps turn red.

The sequence is reversed when going from red to green, if one at all is interested in showing yellow in between.

Imagine, that with the same three colours and three light fixtures, one can triple the awareness and thereby the safety wherever a traffic light is in use.

Completely free to program any sequence adaptable to the various needs, should make them desirable.

Now it's only a question if anyone else already have thought about this?

It would actually be quite strange if that isn't the situation, but for the case of order I have sent this reflection to my patent office, for them to shed light on the situation.

George Manus Valle del Este, South Spain Feb 2016

Trip to Rome in 1958

April 2017

The starting point for this weekend trip was Florence.

The time was around Easter in 1958, just before I terminated my commercial training at Olivetti's school in Florence. I had laid behind me the technical education at Olivetti's factories in Ivrea in the North of Italy the past year and was, according to myself, quite knowledgeable about the language and the culture.

The school was situated in Via Bolognese 106, an impressive estate with parks and buildings, as the one I stayed in, Villa Natalia, from the middle of the nineteenth century.

The Vespa scooter I bought when I first arrived Ivrea in 1956, I had already, after having got my Italian driver licence on my birthday May 14th 57, substituted with a Lancia Aprilia 1949 model.

It had a four cylinder V engine, 1,496 cc with 48 bhp, but don't you think it was slow in the traffic.

In Italy it went under the name: La "Regina della Strada", meaning: "The Queen of the road".

Contrary to the technical school which had many international pupils in addition to the Italians, there were only a few in Florence. It thus became logical that I kept most contact with those coming from Olivetti's subsidiary's and dealers, mainly in Italy.

I no longer remember any names from the school, but on this special occasion tree Italians and myself had, Thursday afternoon packed a minimum of necessities for a two-night's stay-over, in our respective bags.

For the occasion I had purchased a road map which we studied together, to be able to choose what we thought was the best route.

Don't forget that we are back in 1958, almost 60 years ago. Motorways did not exist in those days, but that of course one knew.

My iPad tells me that the flying distance from Florence to Rome is 234 km, and that the distance with car today is 279 km.

I could imagine that in those days, on good old roads, the distance would be well passed 300 km. In other words, the trip should take between four and five hours.

Sparkled with enthusiasm and ready, we set off South this Friday morning.

None of us had earlier been to Rome, so we were all ready for an exciting weekend. We had a minimum of money between us and had not been thinking about accommodation once we were there, that we would deal with on the spot.

Magnificent nature through Toscana led us through several villages which in themselves would have been an experience to explore, and which later in my life I have had the opportunity to do.

Apart from a few natural stops we just kept going, as we had a clear mission.

On a long straight stretch with only scattered gatherings of trees, we can far away see a car parked in our direction. I slowly break and stop behind what turned out to be a green Renault. Before registering that four people were sitting in the car, I got a glimpse of the license plate which was French.

When they discovered that we had stopped behind them, the doors opened and out came four girls, all but one with blond hair. Not typical French I thought with pleasure, as French for me was and is a no spoken language.

It turned out they were all American, touring Europe in a rented car starting from Paris.

The car had just stopped and would not start again.

My three friend didn't speak English, had no feeling for cars, and none of the girls spoke Italian, so logically it was up to me to take the lead.

Of course we would help them.

Their goal for the day was like ours, to reach Rome, after a stop they had made in Siena.

Tank half full, no problem there. Debris in the carburettor was a well-known phenomenon in those days, and the only diagnosis I could think of. The carburettor and air-filter was easy accessible.

Every ting with cars was much simpler in those days, more transparent, making it easier to orientate one-self in the motor department.

Of course, I had my tool kit in the car, so in a short time the air-filter was removed, the carburettor blown clean, and the car started at the first try.

No limits for gratitude. They offered to pay for the help, and told they had booked rooms in a hotel not far from the railway station in Rome.

Of course we could not let them pay, and of course we could not let them alone in this dangerous world, even if they now could continue by themselves.

I made it clear that we would see them well and safe to Rome, as we were anyhow going the same way, and manoeuvred our self in safe distance behind them.

Everything went well, the Renault seemed to be working fine, and late into the afternoon we got them well installed in their hotel.

The language abilities of my Italian friends and the fact that we were short of money, prevented us from further appointments.

After having exchanged addresses and with all good wishes for a pleasant stay and continuous trip back to America, we left them.

It was already dark and we were in the middle of Rome.

My friends suggested we should drive down to the Mediterranean and spend the night there. They had heard about beach parties with open fireplaces, taking place during the weekends.

Good idea I thought without having consulted the map.

In heavy traffic it took us about two hours to finally reach the beach, but, right enough, plenty of fireplaces, people and a whole lot of life.

Full speed from the very first moment.

Way into the morning hours we stumbled into the car, one in each seat, and didn't wake up before the sun long past, had presented another lovely sunny day, at least for those not having partied the whole night.

Having had our late morning swim and prepared for the day the best we could, we headed back to Rome.

What was left of the Saturday we spent taking in one enormous impression after the other without today remembering much of the details.

That has been good for visits to Rome later in life.

In one or another way we again got contact with the girls and met them for a short drink.

After a second evening concentrating on getting as much out of it as possible, I have a recollection that we spent the night in one of the half arches in the Colosseum.

Having been to Rome several times later I understand that doing so today would be totally impossible with much stricter demands for security than in 1958.

Sunday morning originates followed by visits to more attractions, where, after late in the afternoon we leave the city heading North towards Florence – another school day tomorrow.

Unnecessary to mention that we didn't get many hours sleep the last two nights

The first to three hours goes fine. All four are reminiscing about our experiences the last two days.

After a while the pauses between the posts become longer and longer, until I discover that my three friends have fallen asleep.

The radio is turned on, and luckily, I find a station with soft, but not too soft music.

Very little traffic on the road at this time, close to midnight.

The reason why it got so late was a stop we made for something to eat soon after we started.

No denying I am tired, very tired, but I am determined and conscience that I must not fall asleep at the wheel.

I think I have forgotten to mention that I am the only one with a driver license.

All thoughts concentrating on driving carefully and keeping the eyes open – wide open, steering into the beam of the front lights.

The road ahead is the only place lit, as on all sides it's black – eyes are kept wide open.

The music helps and I feel fine.

I estimate to be home in an hour – eyes wide open.

We reach a hilly part. It may be something I feel, as it is pitch dark outside apart from the beam of the front lights. It doesn't help there is no border marking the transition between the earth and the sky either – eyes wide open, full control.

Out in the front a few hundred meters away, the road make a slight turn to the left.

Suddenly it's as if the landscape all around is lit up, so much that the beams from the front light have no meaning. On both sides, I can see no ending yellow meadows, and the road has disappeared.

The brain is sharp – eyes wide open – what's happening?

Completely conscious and calm. The brain commands the right foot to move slowly from the accelerator to the brake pedal. I did not give the order for it to happen.

The brain completely sharp – eyes wide open and hands on the wheel.

The brake pedal is slowly activated while the landscape is still lit up and the road is nowhere to be seen. I am fully conscientious about this.

At the same moment the car came to a standstill, the light disappeared and everything again turned pitch dark, while the beams of the front light again hit the road in front, which until this moment had been non existing.

In the middle of the slight curve we have come to a standstill on the right side of the road.

Still sitting with wide open eyes, I register that the other three are still sleeping.

As I wake them, I tell them I need a little pause.

After a breath of fresh air, I tell them that from now on until we are home there will be no sleeping, their task should be to keep me awake.

They remind happily ignorant about my experience until we had the lunch break after the first ours at school. Needless to say, they looked somewhat confused when I told them, but I'm convinced, that if they still live they will as me remember this weekend in Rome in 1958.

Personally, I think this event is a proof of how the will of the brain can take over control, when the motoric fails due to over fatigue.

Of course I will never recommend anyone to calculate with that to happen.

Truth

Mars 2014

When you hear the expression «The truth is….», then be on the alert.

Everyone using this phrase, after my opinion lacks understanding of realities.

The one using the expression "The truth is…", and not instantly adds "after my opinion", is lacking any form of credibility.

What is true and what's not, unfortunately for many, is a stretchy concept.

The expression "the truth is…" is just as hopeless as described in an earlier reflection which was named "To be honest…". (Reflections II).

It's easy to mix the use of the words truth and honesty. In many ways, they go together, but of course does not.

I never heard anyone say: "This is my honest truth". If that was the case, the reason must have been to underline the truth.

Think about it. In this case, first one emphasize one's "honesty", underlining one's general honest. Second one make the mistake of stating the "Truth" unconditionally. The truth for whom?

Typically, this case demands an amendment as for example: "Subjectively, this is my honest truth.

Anyhow, after my opinion, it's nevertheless a big difference between the words truth and honesty.

The "truth", even daily being treated sloppily by many, is of course not stretchy, it's black or white. Either it is true or it's not true, or false.

That should be obvious, but who possesses the "right truth", and then what about the "right truth".

Here we are facing the incorrect truth and the correct truth.

The closest example I can come up with – to put this "incorrect truth and the correct truth" in a more understandable light for us all - is to have a look at the media. Probably today's most dominating media regarding news and information, is the TV.

Of course there is also the written press together with a lot of social media more and more used in conjunction with modern technology.

This however is much to comprehensive to deal with in a little reflection like this.

I stick to the TV, and imagine that there must be tenth of thousands of TV channels available in the world.

No use to touch the countries working with only state controlled TV. There of course, after my opinion, the "correct truth" never reaches the population.

With tenth of thousands of channels it's obvious there are equally many influencing possibilities.

Only within the EU there are more than 6000 channels available.

It's not as if they all transmit news of course, or in any way perform conscious influence on us viewers, but within all genera it focuses on "truth".

Some of them likes to be the carrier of "truth", and others claim they are the one presenting the "correct truth".

I will limit myself to one example which I in return think is quite engraving.

No reason to hide which channel I'm referring to – CNN. By all means a news channel, and the one claiming they are the largest in the world.

Here I got to know by one of the top journalists, in an advertisement to promote the channel, that she had a new twist on her reporting, she was going to tell the "truth". Important for us listeners to know.

As far as I remember it was taken off after a few months having been continually repeated, so obviously someone must have discovered the blunder.

The essential when dealing with the "truth", after my opinion, is that one sees it in conjunction with objectivity.

The one, or those claiming that their channel represents the "correct truth" must, if they look for credibility, emphasize that they present their information's based on their own objective reviews.

It means that they have judged the "truth" of the information's in question from the outside, put themselves in a position to objectively look at all sides of the case.

One thing is the objective attitude towards the "truth", but does one have time to go into all the details, and is it really that important?

The news comes first they say, and of course it's important to be the first.

Correctness, meaning the "truth". Yes, of course it's important that what's presented is "true", but at the same time it's even more important that the number of viewers are kept and increased?

This happens only if the public feel that the channel in question is delivering.

The fact that an enormous number of channels are available must not be forgotten. Many of them transmitting content where the "truth" is not looked upon as being important?

May it be that all channels on TV have their own norms regarding the "truth", and that they are based on the owner's assumptions, political attitude and economic interests?

What happens to the "truth" in the middle of all this?

So, called "authentic reports" must also be mentioned.

"Authentic" defines as something genuine, original or something having its own character. Nothing is mentioned about "truth", and that's maybe not necessary?

Maybe it's easier for the TV companies to identify themselves with the "authentic" form of "truth". Is that "truth" more tolerant than the general "truth"?

One's political attitude, I believe, logically decides which channels one prefer, often based on the kind of "truth "they represents and one believe in.

The expression: "The truth may be in between" may for many seem logical, but does anyone believe that if one take news from RT (Russian Television) and CNN and divide them in two, one gets the correct "truth"? Maybe an extreme example as I have understood that the RT channel is state controlled?

Could there be anything in that: "the origin of truth, the source, can be the truths worst enemy"?

Unfortunately, nothing in the world can be ideal, so maybe one must accept the "truth" we are faced with in daily life, and use our common senses?

UFO

2013

The term UFO stands for Unidentified Flying Object or what is popularly called a flying saucer. In this case, the abbreviation also works for the Norwegian translation "Uidentifiserbare Flygende Objekter". However, don't draw the conclusion from this that it is a Norwegian invention, even though the English expression could have been translated directly from Norwegian.

No reason to dwell too much on it though.

One either believes that there is more between Heaven and Earth than one knows about and sees it as not being an impossibility for a form of life out there to be capable of visiting us here on earth or at least observing us from above. Or, one has made it clear to oneself that it is nothing but hogwash or optical illusions, when from time to time a sighting of an UFO has been reported. There have even been claims made that several of them visited us thousands of years ago, forming other civilizations here on earth which have since disappeared.

All the different speculations about this subject are of no interest to me as long as no concrete evidence exists; no, for me the whole thing seems a lot simpler.

If it is so that Our Lord has created the universe, I don't believe us wranglers here on earth would be the only form of intelligence He'd place His bets on. For all we know, we might end up destroying all life as we know it, ourselves included, and then what?

If there is no other form of life in the universe, would this be the end of everything? No, of course, it can't be like that. I don't think there are only a few, but an infinite number of life forms out there, where, as far as us humans can agree on, there are no limits.

Many have experiences to look back on as far as this subject goes and a great number of books have been written about it, either claiming authenticity or as works of science fiction.

I don't know if my experience back in the seventies was observed by anyone else, as I wasn't able to stop and digest the event there and then.

On my way home from the office in my red Chevrolet station wagon one summer afternoon, something happened which was the closest I've been to a UFO experience.

Traffic as far as the eye can see in both directions and in both lanes of Trondheimsveien down toward the ring road, which is to take me westward to where I live in Vettakollen. Despite the traffic, the queue is moving exceptionally well and since its Friday, I'm thinking about the evening's BBQ, with a few good friends, and what I know is missing to make it perfect. I'm planning to stop at Gullkroken to shop for the last-minute ingredients.

With nothing but blue sky everywhere it looks like it'll be a super weekend.

Twenty or thirty meters to the car in front and the same to the one behind and a speed of about seventy kilometres an hour.

Suddenly, for no reason whatsoever, I look up towards the sky way ahead of me and high above car roofs. There I spot what to me looks like what I associate with a flying saucer.

Aluminium coloured and circle shaped, flat on the bottom and with a curved upper part. That it rotates I can see from what looks like round windows in the upper part.

Get a bit of a shock at first, but I'm still conscious enough to think about keeping my speed up as well as the distance to the car in front and, not least, to stay in the middle of the lane.

As often as I can I look up at the saucer, which gradually, and as if in slow-motion becomes bigger and bigger. It seems to stay at the same altitude.

Is it coming towards me or is it only getting bigger because I, as all the other cars, am getting closer?

No one else seems to have noticed the phenomenon as the queue keeps moving at the same speed. It's possible, of course, that others have discovered the phenomenon but dare not apply the brakes because of the consequences this might lead to. A panic reaction like that could easily cause a chain collision.

It suddenly looks like the saucer, which has turned a bit toward the left, seen from my angle, turns once more to the right, again seen from my angle, loses height and is coming straight toward me.

Seconds later it turns more and more into a horizontal position at the same time as it, very quickly, increases in size.

With my foot on the accelerator exerting the same pressure as before and with a firm grip on the steering wheel, I unconsciously duck down as a great bang is heard. When I, a moment later, as a reaction to the bang, again raise my head, I see a gigantic hub-cap bounce up where the windscreen meets the roof directly above the steering wheel and disappear from the lane on the right.

As if nothing has happened, the queue keeps moving along Trondheimsveien at the same speed and at the same distance as before.

When I've pulled myself together and recapitulated what has happened, it horrifies me to think of what would have happened if it had hit only twenty centimetres lower.

When I say that it was a gigantic hub-cap, the reason for it became clear when I overtook an enormous lorry on the left and saw that the hub-cap on the back pair of wheels was missing. From the cap on the pair of wheels next to it, I saw that the diameter must have been close to a meter and that the windows I'd seen were holes forming a circle around its centre.

What had made the hub-cap fall off and what it had hit to make it "fly" the way it did, I can't say, but it became a memorable experience, albeit not as strong as it would have been if I had encountered a real UFO.

After all, there were no little green men involved in this case.

Before I enter Gullkroken to do my shopping, I take a look at the damages, of course. It was a wonder that the windscreen hadn't been broken.

As though the wound had been caused by a giant axe, the cut was more than twenty centimetres long and several centimetres deep, but fortunately so far forward that the metal beam above the windscreen had caught the brunt of it.

I believe it must have been the first and last time the insurance agent was faced with car damage caused by a collision with a flying saucer.

Understanding

2017

The wish of understanding and will to understand is fundamental. If one wishes not to understand or rejects the thought of understanding, no understanding is achieved and consequently one can't expect to be understood either. One must have the wish and will to understand, to achieve understanding. In other words, understanding requires both wish and will.

Does one come further with understanding?

After my opinion undoubtedly yes.

All decisions, if they should have any validity, must be based on understanding, and the wish and will to understand the content of the matter and the parties involved.

In many cases, it is much easier to keep the understanding in the background, not to use will, force and time to understand. Then, however the probability is great for the decisions to be of poor quality.

Imagine that it is so simple.

Pundits are normally easy to understand. They often express simple understandable postulates about this and that, but thanks to their personality they are normally categorised as unsympathetic.

Those, who on the other side acts consciously and keep the more modest style will normally be both respected and appreciated.

"Do you understand"? An expression often used when one expects a confirmation that the message is understood.

After my opinion too much on the commanding side. One take it for granted that the message is understood. A yes is expected as a confirmation.

For many it becomes difficult to say no, even if that is what they mean. For the one party this is of course correct, but what about the quality of the understanding.

Why not try with a little more weekend question? "I hope you have understood". This gives full admission to grasp eventual insecurity, and may result in the following answer: "Yeas, but I have a few questions". The dialogue is on, understanding substantiated, the communication is balanced and basis laid for a compromised result.

Nit-picking many will say, especially in this times with SMS and mail where the most advanced communicators uses a minimum of words with associated probability of misunderstandings.

These days one even have reached so far as for some TV channels to squeeze the information or message into one line. To achieve this all kind of abbreviations are used, making it meaningless for us ordinary people. What happened to the understanding? Well, the one that understand that?

Most probably, only us in "the vintage age" are the ones who sighs. Every now and then, in debates, one will recognise someone testing the following entry as an answer to a statement.

"I have a great deal of understanding for what you are saying, but......."

Well, I suppose it won't last long before also this expression disappears. It's much easier saying it directly: "I disagree with what you are saying".

I hope for some understanding of my view on the importance of understanding.

We are all different

Jan. 2017

Only when we admit that we are different and are willing to take that debate, are we capable to form a just and viable democracy.

Of course, it's more popular, to say that we are all alike, it's more solidarity and security in it. That democracy implies that we are all alike in relation to law and regulations, is both obvious and just, and that we are equipped with the same amount of legs, arms, ears and eyes, situated the same place on our body, are clear equality features.

That we come in two different issues in form of female and male, we luckily take for granted.

When I claim that we humans aren't alike, I don't talk about groups, colour of skin, religious beliefs and such.

We all have our complete and unique identity. Whether it's about DNA, fingerprint or other forms of identification, none of us on the entire planet are alike.

Shouldn't that give a good explanation of why expressions like: "we are all alike", not only are wrong, but totally misleading.

After my opinion that is one of the most misguiding lies we are growing up with. Humans have never been, and will never be alike.

Those predicting that we are all alike, and that we as a consequence therefore is expected to behave accordingly are, after my opinion completely on the wrong trail.

If the Creator had meant that we should all be alike, well, then he would never equip us with our unique individual identity.

The Creator didn't make this complicated curvature, to make us all unique if he meant that we should all be alike.

The fact that we all are different is of course the reason why we in one or another form always compete. This goes for us all, we all compete, consciously or unconsciously.

If we had all been alike the motive of competition would be lost, and the consequences of that would have been that we would have remained at the Stone Age level, if at all we would have been created.

Why should we have been created as humans if it wasn't meant that we should develop? Wouldn't that have been totally meaningless? It's a fact that development only happens when competition is stimulated.

Whatever our faith, creation must have a meaning.

What I really want to emphasize is that the myth about us all being alike must get a total twist, for the world not to stop. We must turn the tide, and fully accept competition on all levels. If we do that we at the same time accepts that we basically are different – and we are on the right track.

Realism must be cultivated and get a meaningful place in the society, not as today where realism in many ways is looked upon as a bad word.

There is no form of racism in this, but a foundation for human survival.

Respect and tolerance must get a renewed importance and value. Values in general must be revised.

Reason suggests that a much to big part of the population is trapped by the political dogma that we are all alike and consequently should be treated the same way. After my opinion it should go like this:

We are all different and unique and thus should be treated respectfully.

Our social system should function in a way that respects us as the different individuals we are, and give us opportunities to develop individually.

We must not be forced into certain forms by rules and laws, that will turn out completely wrong and create great opposites. Changing attitudes must be voluntary.

Obviously, this require new thinking and greater demand must be made to society and business.

In all contexts it's proven that everything depends on the leadership, and that this is the challenge.

Who should rule and decide is the question, and who should control that it happens within the rules and in a transparent and just manner?

The concepts of justice must be made crystal clear and demand for fair leadership must be sharpened.

Democracy is so far, anyway by us in the societies we belong to in the west, the system giving the best compromise for just leadership.

In a democracy it's people, through their right of voting, who decide the political outcome – and that's the way it should be.

I really never believed in the "enlightened one ruler system", even if it would be perfect if it would work in a just way.

However, the reason it doesn't work, and never will, is just because we are different.

The one who eventually should be the "enlightened one ruler" would be one of us, with the same strengths and weaknesses, meaning that the system could never work.

Knight Svend on his horse - Jan Arnt 2010

With my back against the wall

Mars 1991

 The best for me is that the year 1990 is over.

I am convinced that all of us at least once in our life time have experienced things we would rather be without.

Many of us have surely been through great trials, with reactions as many and varied as the situations.

Unwanted challenges and tragedies are thrown upon one like lightening from a clear sky when least expected, and one is forced to relate realistically to the circumstances.

At times I have heard from people who have experienced difficult challenges, that they have felt stronger having gone through their experiences.

"It's a heck of a shame that one has to go through difficulties to feel good". This phrase I believe we have all heard and I feel sure I'm not alone in my reaction.

Although I always got the point and thought I'd understood, and to a certain extent have been able to identify myself with the difficult situation of others, I can today see that I didn't have the foggiest idea and no prerequisite to understand.

In my opinion it is only through one's own experiences and the way one relates to adversity, that one can understand and thereby have a qualified meaning about a case.

My business challenges which started with a downturn in our industry at the beginning of 1988 only turned worse. The challenges at times looked invincible.

It was very difficult to see the light in the tunnel and my thoughts had been spinning in a hint of egoism, mostly related to these business challenges.

About myself I have always meant that I by nature don't see to many difficulties and that I mostly relate to problems as being challenges.

It's been a lot of comfort that one hasn't been alone with the challenges and it's been easy to find situations one could identify with and understand.

In this period I was never in doubt that adversity in the end would give strength. When the general economy finally picked up, those who had managed to consolidate would stay strong in the marketplace.

Just before Christmas 89, a message came as light from the clear sky, my daughter Nicoline at 26 was seriously ill.

The feeling of helplessness I got then made all business challenges fade. A switch was turned on and life got a whole new content.

With incredible strength, she lived an almost full life until she well a year later, in January '90 had to give up.

A little more than one year has elapsed since she passed away, and only now, tree years after the business challenges started, it seems like circumstances are on the way to stabilize.

The time during her illness and not the least the grief after her has been heavy to bear, but in a strange way I feel today more of a "whole" person.

Undoubtedly a few concepts have become clearer to me, concepts which were earlier hanging in the air.

Values are drastically changed, expressions like "to appreciate", have got a new meaning and the term "tolerance" has got a renewed content.

I now know that adversity can give optimism and challenges pleasure.

However, with the assumption that one constantly focuses on one's positive sides.

Personally, I don't believe, as is said, that time does heal all wounds, but that we all can learn to live with deep wounds by dealing with them property.

You are alone

12 June 2015

This is not a statement about you being alone in the sense of not having family or friends close to you and loving you. A reasonably long experience has given me reasons to feel that I have both family and friends which appreciate me, so in the context of solitude I don't feel alone. The meaning of feeling alone I have in mind, is related to a challenge I am convinced quite a few of us have been facing.

At a certain time, in different contexts, you reach a point, or rather a top, from which one normally can just look down to find an answer.

Why one only looks down is logical, because it's only down there one can see the tangible realities, as it's normally there one has gained ones experiences. If one looks up there is just nothing.

In daytime the impression one gets can be grey and sad, but also bright and clear when the sun shines from a bright heaven.

The expression: "Over the clouds, the sun always shines", is a good reminder to lift the spirit a little.

If it's night and overcast it's black, but if the night's cloudless you see endless amounts of stars, and often the moon as the largest light source.

For many, the answer to versatile challenges in life lies up there, whatever faith.

Many govern their life related to the contact they feel they have up there, independent of their religion.

For those it matters, it becomes okay and easy I should think, even if the faith can be put to great tests.

Personally I have had my fair part of challenges throughout life, and have as one of my slogans:

"It's mainly through challenges and how you tackle them, you learn to advance.

What relation each of us have to prayer must be kept as a private matter".

As my daughter and son in law took over the responsibility of the company, naturally enough it became him being confronted with unforeseen challenges

He has a strong robust attitude to most, and tackles his position impeccably.

I seldom give advice unless questioned, but one thing I from the beginning tried to convey to him based on my own experience. Whatever good employees you have, it will guaranteed and more often than you think, occur situations where you are alone, it is up to you to take the final decision and there is no one you can ask but yourself.

As a result of that it's also you having to take the consequences from your decisions.

Situations will occur where only you, for good reasons have all information's as they can't be shares with anyone.

That's what comes with being a responsible leader.

My son in law have on several occasions faced challenges where I reminded him about this, but so far I have a certain impression of that not being necessary. I think he is aware of that matter and have a good understanding about the situation.

Many reading this might not totally understand or agree that it is like this. Rightly, from their point of view they feel being valuable supporters, as by all means they are.

The same goes for board members. In the same way, they feel they have the job, amongst other because they give good advices. They also, from their point of view do believe they are good advisers, and of course they are.

But, and that is an important but – as I believe only can be understood by the ones with the ultimate responsibility: "Occasions will occur where you stand totally alone".

The Trip

December 2012

Everyone has their own experiences and adventures when travelling. It is here as with so many other things in life, no one escapes, it just depends how the incident presents itself. For some it goes far beyond just adventures and experiences, but even far more serious things are only worldly and when it comes down to it, can usually be remedied quite simply.

In our case on this special occasion, it all ended well, but it was an experience with a somewhat unusual twist.

I can't help mentioning names where praise is deserved, but will remain indirect whenever it required an effort to keep one's shirt on in issues involving discrimination or worse.

Everything started with our getting ready to go on our annual trip to Denmark in December in connection with a board meeting and other business activities.

Copenhagen is well worth a visit in December with its famous pedestrian streets decorated for Christmas, its people in a festive mood and its many pleasant restaurants to visit.

All this is actually immaterial to the context which concerns the trip itself.

A trip means, as we normally experience it, to get from one place to another and at some later stage, return to the starting point.

The times of departure and arrival at this time of year don't depend on your wishes but on the available offers.

We were leaving home, which is the South of Spain, for Copenhagen and coming back after a short week's stay.

The only possibility or rather what suited us best, was with Norwegian from Alicante, via Oslo, to Copenhagen.

Our return was a direct flight with the same airline from Copenhagen to Alicante, however with a late departure and even later arrival; at almost midnight.

In Copenhagen we stayed at an impeccable hotel.

On December the fifth we left home at eight o'clock in the morning. Had beautiful sunshine all the way and arrived at the airport more than two hours before departure.

First the rows from 16 on are to be filled and that's fine. We had booked in advance at the emergency exit and waited until those behind took their seats.

While this is taking place, an enormous example of the female species wanders around yelling abuse at people. It's quite clear to me that this is a person who through her "power" is taking revenge for I don't know what. It's all well and good that there are rules for what one is allowed to bring on board the plane and that it in this case had been made clear over the loudspeakers that the plane was full. One poor man carrying a rucksack and two modest soft plastic bags is downright scolded and practically told to get lost. One passenger after the other was told in no uncertain terms that if they didn't check in their hand-luggages and shopping bags, they could forget about their trip.

She was probably Spanish and I don't blame Norwegian Air Shuttle. To have someone like that on the payroll would be a disgrace for the employer. Just think how easy it would be for the person in question to explain with a smile that this and that bag would have to be moved to the bottom of the plane due to lack of space, if the person deserved his or her job that is.

A Norwegian elderly woman next to me said in a loud, clear voice something like:

I thought the time of the Gestapo was in the past.

The representative of the female race in question was the perfect image of someone in a story from the German concentration camps.

Well, that was that. Rather exhausted we finally found our seats and after more than 7 hours, having had a stopover in Oslo, we arrived at Kastrup airport in Copenhagen.

As I've already said, our stay has nothing to do with this story, so we'll get straight to the point.

In a howling blizzard, check-out from the hotel has been delayed until 2 p.m. The plane wasn't to leave until 8 p.m. But what could we do in such terrible weather?

A taxi directly to Kastrup with a wait of more than 5 hours.

The check-in takes place at a machine after which the luggage is put on the conveyor belt.

The above mentioned episode on our departure has left its marks; perhaps such people are what's needed to make us follow the rules? I hope not.

Both my wife and I have our small, approved hand-luggage. She also has, like almost all women, an additional purse. This, as I've been made to understand after the episode, is absolutely forbidden.

We also normally buy plenty of reading material, which I on this occasion carried in a plastic bag along with two small bottles of water.

Conscientious as I am, I agree with my wife that I don't need anything from the hand-luggage during the flight, so we check it in as luggage item number two.

My wife had put my iPad in her purse along with her own, since we'd heard for the first time that we could use them while in the air.

With a clear conscience we wander over to security control to start getting "undressed" for the body search. This has become quite stressful for us who are well into our seventies, but one gets used to most things.

On the way I realize that I've left the car keys in my hand-luggage, so I jokingly say to my wife: the only thing missing now is for it not to get to Alicante. That's where we've left our car, which will take us the last 200 kilometres to our home.

We then concentrate on how to pass the time until 8 o'clock and don't give it another thought. We have a late lunch knowing that it'll be the last meal of the day.

After a half hour delay due to the incoming plane's late arrival, we're in the air with a three hour flight ahead of us.

Everything's perfect with a friendly crew. The purser is wearing a Santa hat, and everyone smiling left and right.

We land in Alicante more or less on time at half past eleven but find that here the sun has set in more than one way.

We normally prefer the lift to the escalator these days, but no such luck. The red lights are on everywhere, at both lifts and escalators.

We carefully make our way down the stairs to the baggage claim; it's fortunately not so that we are unable to manage this.

Most of the lights had been turned off and apart from two policemen, we saw no one.

Yes indeed, even at quite a distance we could see our red suitcase which was a good sign, and my wife's hand-luggage. Mine however, was more difficult to find.

After everything became dead and silent, we still hadn't found it; good advice would now come at a price.

A sweet and friendly airport employee, who turned out to be responsible for "lost and found", suddenly appeared pulling three suitcases.

She explained that they had a delay of two days, also from Copenhagen. When we explained our situation, she got the policemen to search outside the arrivals hall as well as the luggage conveyance machinery itself.

When they had no luck finding it, she registered my hand-luggage as missing in a charming and professional way. Her name is Sandra Mira and she works for Menzies Aviation, which I expect is part of the airport administration.

So there we are, without a key to the car, wandering slowly as the very last ones out of the arrivals hall which at this point is lit only by emergency lights.

Luckily there are still a couple of taxis left, one of which when requested takes us to the Melia Hotel in Alicante.

It had been an incredibly long day which culminated in getting into bed totally exhausted at half past one in the morning.

A pleasant breakfast at 10 o'clock got our brain windings working again and we set off back to the airport in a taxi.

At the office responsible for Norwegian Air Schuttle, the said Menzies Aviation but this time in the departure hall itself, another helpful woman came to our aid.

After just a short time it became clear that the hand-luggage hadn't been found anywhere but that the first plane from Copenhagen would arrive that evening at the same time we had arrived the night before. While we were sitting there on a bench close to the Ryanair check-in counter waiting for the woman to investigate, I saw to my consternation the same dragon that had made her performance the week before, on the day we were leaving.

I checked the departure board and saw that she was handling the passengers who were going to Santiago on FR 8538 at 12:55.

After having dealt with a customer, as the person in question was leaving the counter carrying or pulling his or her hand-luggage, I saw her glaring at them and measuring their size with her eyes. Could another victim be punished?

My aversion against the person grew, but I set it all aside thinking about what we had to do.

The only logical thing would be to hire a car, which we promptly did, and set off for home.

After a couple of hours, around two o'clock, we arrived home. My wife had the keys to the flat, so all was well so far.

Half an hour later they phoned from the airport to tell us that the hand-luggage had been found in Copenhagen and that it would be on the plane arriving at midnight.

The question was where to deliver it?

As we had explained before leaving the airport, it was out of the question for us to wait there for twelve hours that day, in the hope that it would arrive, and that we had thus hired a car. This I would bring back to the airport the following day as I had to pick up our car anyway and would then pick up the hand-luggage at the same time.

Delivery was thus uninteresting and they could save themselves the expense of a four hour drive.

With the return trip to Alicante, to pick up our car and the hand-luggage, I had in twenty-four hours covered four hundred kilometres more than I would have had to if had accompanied us.

Collecting the hand-luggage I found that it was completely ruined. It looked like it had been "put through the grinder", but luckily everything was there, including the car key, even though the zip of the pocket it was in had been ripped off.

The incredibly helpful woman in "lost and found" wrote a report and everything seemed ready for my writing a claim to the airline.

I won't bother the readers with the details around all that, but could make a few remarks.

Norwegian Air Schuttle, to whom I, in my opinion, sent a detailed report, drew my attention to the fact that they weren't responsible for any luggage content whatsoever and that their liability was restricted to a maximum of 500 NOK for a damaged suitcase. (500 NOK = +- 70 Euro).

Should there be any kind of compensation, the bag in question would have to be sent to them for evaluation.

I had also enclosed an invoice for the hotel accommodation in Alicante, the taxi and the one day car hire.

The total came to about two thousand Norwegian kroner, (+-280 Euro).

This was also not their responsibility. That they had been saved a four hundred kilometre trip to deliver the bag was, of course, forgotten.

Just the frustration and the work associated with making the report, plus the driving to and from the airport greatly exceeds the amount in question, but one thing is certain and that is that one can chalk one up, to experience having been through a situation like this one.

Apart from all that, it was a wonderful week.

The Typewriter

May 2013

This story is for me so special and full of details that it could probably form the basis for a reasonably thick book. It would in that case definitely only have been of interest to a selected few, so I will attempt a strong concentration, a condensed version, which one hopefully doesn't get bored with. The only time-description I can vouch for as being accurate is when the original idea was formed.

The year is 1957 and I find myself in the South of Europe, that is to say at Olivetti's technical school in Ivrea in Northern Italy. I am to be trained to instruct our mechanics in the repair of all types of typewriters and calculators.

Max Manus Office Machines owned by my step-father, represented at that time, among others, the office machine giant, Olivetti, in Norway and since all the machines were mechanical, the electronic age had not yet been invented, a large part of the company employees were mechanics.

Contrary to today's technology the machines had to have regular inspections and maintenance in order to perform properly.

A number of different models of both typewriters and calculators had to be known down to their ultimate screws, a demanding but interesting task, as the most complicated calculators consisted of several thousand different parts.

The typewriters caught my interest especially and then in particular the electrical ones. They consisted of a number of mechanical connections from the key to the type bar, the part that puts the letter imprint on the paper. I got the idea that all this could be simplified and improved.

After countless hours in the hotel room after school and having looked at a variety of solutions to the challenge, I arrived at the one that seemed the easiest, that was to attack the type bar directly without using mechanical connectors. Electrical impulses, directly from the keystroke could, by activating a small electromagnet, select the chosen type bar, after which a universal striking rail controlled by a solenoid (a type of electromagnet) would put this in motion toward the ribbon and the paper. The electrical impulses from the keys could at the same time in a desired form be stored for instance on a magnetic tape, to be played back later. I believe we called it automatic writing.

Most of the technical stuff should thus be covered in the simplest possible manner.

I saw the principle itself quite clearly, but could do nothing practical about it for as long as I went to school, I was after all going back to Norway at some point to instruct our mechanics.

None the less my thoughts returned constantly to this principle and I quickly understood that here knowledge was needed which lay far beyond my range at the time.

Back in Norway instructions got under way and with close to forty own mechanics and a network of thirty dealerships and five subsidiaries' throughout the country, there was enough to do.

Several return trips were made to Ivrea for updates on new models.

The manager of our technical department for dictation machines, Torbjørn Myrvold, a first class precision mechanic, who worked under the same roof as I, was quickly made aware of my ideas and we put together a working principle model with three keys and three type bars.

It soon became clear that Torbjørn's detailed knowledge when it came to the new world of electronics, which we could all see coming, was far from what was required in order to construct the electronic part of a complete functional model.

How to acquire this knowledge? In our department of Loudspeaking Intercom Systems, there turned out to be an employee who had actually learnt about the new wonder, the transistor, at Oslo Technical Institute.

His name was Bjørn Andersen. He was my age but, thanks to his knowledge he already had responsibility for the technical side of the department. I hardly knew the word transistor, but understood at an early stage that without using them and the technology surrounding them, my idea could not be realized.

My step-father, Max, had early on been introduced to the principle model and with his sporty attitude and nose for possibilities, he immediately agreed that it had to be developed further and we were already in the process of applying for a patent. This turned out to be more of an on-going process than a one-time action, something I have later experienced in spades.

However, there ended up being several patents to do with the principle.

On to plans and action. Everything had to be kept secret and all three of us had, of course, to maintain full working days at our respective departments, so it was a question of finding unorthodox solutions.

We rented premises at Grensen 9, just a stone's throw away from Karl Johans gate 21, where our firm's head offices were located and where the department for Intercom Systems where Bjørn worked, was based. Torbjørn and I worked at our premises in Etterstad where the firm's other technical departments were situated.

We must all have been very keen on the idea of exploring all facets of this new typewriter concept and got going with great optimism. At the end of the working day, each from his job, we rushed to the hot-dog kiosk at the corner, before going to Grensen 9, where we often worked until close to midnight.

The time to come was a great strain on the home-front for all of us and especially for Torbjørn, it became over time, thanks to our diet, a bit much for his stomach. He was after all a good ten years older than Bjørn and I.

On the electronic side, Bjørn experimented with a number of different concepts we came up with, for transferring letters to paper. When one is obsessed by the idea of creating something new, it is incredible the number of ideas one has, but that's a different matter as this wasn't to become a book.

The main task was the control of solenoids and electromagnets and the curbing of noise from same.

It wasn't hard to see that Bjørn was an incredible talent within electronics.

Individually each key on the typewriter keyboard had to submit electric impulses to the little electromagnet underneath each type bar, in itself not the simplest of tasks. The electromagnet selected in its turn a small mechanical part on the type bar itself, which milliseconds later was struck by the rail which again was run by a universal solenoid. The theoretical speed was among other things limited by how quickly this solenoid could work.

Bjørn did the pioneering work when it came to slowing down and reversing its movements electronically, both in order to gain speed and to reduce noise. The mechanical part Myrvold was responsible for in as far as the more complicated tasks were concerned, whereas I was there for inspiration and to learn. I mostly ended up working on mechanical solutions which lay outside the basic principle itself and on the production of mechanical parts, we were after all to construct a complete typewriter.

With my inbred interest in technique and Torbjørn as teacher I soon saw myself as a worthwhile member of the team, with Bjørn as a natural authority on electronics.

Thanks to our connections with Philips in Holland as a representative for their dictation machines, they had become interested in our concept and eventually sponsored the construction of the model.

During this time there were several visits to Eindhoven, where Philips had their headquarters and where Bjørn frolicked in their newly developed components within the world of electronics.

We were both in our early twenties at this time, were completely lacking in experience and had blind faith in our project and its success in becoming the world's fastest typewriter.

Our objective was in other words to construct an electromechanical typewriter which would exceed other typewriters by far when it came to speed.

IBM's golf ball typewriter could as output machine, that is to say when controlled by a magnetic tape, type at a speed of 16 strokes a second if I'm not mistaken. Checking it out more closely, the actual speed of an IBM Selectric was 13.4 strokes a second.

The electromechanical principle in our first prototype reached 25 stokes per second, without the principle's possibilities in this context having been in any way fully tested.

There is, however, a long way from model to actual production, incredibly long. I have learnt a lot about that later in life.

I seem to remember that there was a Prof. Dr. Hildebrandt who, in an article in the German magazine, Feinwerktechnik, analysed if a typewriter based on electromechanical transmissions could possibly become a reality. The analysis turned out badly, as he came to the conclusion that one due to heat generation would need a construction which occupied a medium-size room.

With this as part of the reason, the German patent authorities refused initially to grant a patent for the concept.

The complete model was eventually more or less completed and it had already been arranged for us to go to the Philips headquarters in Eindhoven to present the marvel to the top management, which at the time consisted of 28 division directors including Fritz Philips himself.

To kill two birds with one stone, we arranged to meet with the patent authorities in Munich, and with the prototype in a specially put together wooden crate, we set off on the ferry to Kiel. The prototype was built on the frame of an Olivetti typewriter and looked from the outside like an ordinary one, which was far from the case.

After several problems with customs on the German border as well as other memorable episodes which I'll skip, we finally arrived at the patent office in Munich.

Too bad one couldn't have taken a picture of the engineers as they stood there open-mouthed as the machine clattered away at 25 strokes a second.

We knew, of course, that we had some critical limits as far as heat generation was concerned, but that was just peanuts compared to the complex of improvisations and hand-made parts the construction consisted of. Furthermore it was only Bjørn who really understood that part of the challenge.

The patent application was immediately reconsidered and a patent was granted at a later date, also in Germany, in addition to 16 other countries.

The continuation of the trip to Eindhoven began with a breakdown of the gears on the motorway. My little Austin would on the occasion only let itself be moved in the second and fourth gears.

It was a strange feeling to balance between only two gears, especially in big city traffic, but dead tired we finally ended up at the hotel Silveren Seepaerd in Eindhoven close to midnight.

The typewriter was moody, it was after all made only to prove that the principles held, so the mechanism was cleaned until the early hours of the morning, inspected and made ready for the big presentation to take place later the same day.

In second and fourth gears we reached the Philips administration building and were shown to what was called the ELA auditorium. It seemed to me like a cinema, but with a stage instead of a screen. A table in the middle of this stage, was put at our disposal whereupon we under floodlights set everything up. Minutes before the doors opened, two outwardly self-assured young men from Norway stood there in the middle of the stage with only one objective, which was to tell at least 20 of Philips top directors, both technical and commercial, what the future world of typewriters would look like. The sweat was already running as a result of the heat from the floodlights combined with our nervousness.

After a short introduction, I organize a stack of A4 sheets and put carbon paper between each of them. *If this story gets into the hands of today's young people, they'll probably have to look up the meaning of carbon paper.*

I do this in such a way that everyone can see the details and that I at the end place the stack down onto the platen and turn the knob.

I then hold up the Philips dictation machine we used for automatic writing and explain that what I now type will be stored on the tape of the dictation machine, so that we can later print it in context.

There is dead silence in the auditorium as I explain what I'm writing as I'm doing it:

"The quick brown fox jumps over the lazy dog". The entire alphabet is covered in this one sentence. I press the return key on the dictation machine, which in one second rewinds back to its starting position.

I first look at Bjørn, who looks like he's standing in the shower, probably addressing higher powers with a prayer that the heat or for that matter other things won't stop this historical event from becoming a success. I had, of course, during the introduction explained all about IBM's typewriter, the contemporary marvel, and its speed.

After a brrr … , which lasted about a second, there is again dead silence. I turn the roller, and with the stack of papers consisting of sixteen copies in my hand I move towards the front row and start distributing the sheets. As these top directors with responsibility for four hundred thousand employees saw the result, they broke into an unreserved applause.

The typewriter was left at Philips for closer studies and I stayed for further discussions, while Bjørn drove the Austin back to Norway the next day in second and fourth.

For us both this became one of our greatest experiences.

I can't recall how we celebrated the evening after the event.

It remains to be said that a technical director at Philips called up in despair after a while to tell us that the typewriter had broken down.

We were going down there anyway to discuss technical details with them so it would probably work out. Self-assured to the point of stupidity, we have to use our ages as an excuse, we couldn't help ourselves when we were invited for lunch by the same director after Bjørn had got the typewriter working again. He insisted on knowing where the fault had been. Bjørn is not one of the most talkative types, but he had already gained a lot of respect for his technical knowledge from our partner. He puts his hand in his pocket and pulls out a little green plastic box, Philips first integrated circuit, holds it out and says: "In this".

Fortunately it wasn't taken the wrong way nor was it meant to offend.

Philips invested large amounts in further developments but finally decided that they would have to build a completely new typewriter factory in order to put the machine into production. In their initial euphoria they had probably overlooked this detail and they eventually begged off politely.

It was probably characteristic for a company in the category of Philips that they only half a year later bought the German typewriter factory Zimag, but that was in a completely different context and had nothing to do with us.

Both parties were, however, satisfied with the experiences one had made in several areas and which, not least, gave us a lot of self-confidence.

Within the European office machine industry some rumours must have circulated about us, because one day we were visited by the top boss in the Swiss company, Paillard. They produced among others the typewriter, Hermes, along with some very advanced record players and cameras and were situated in the city of Yverdon.

As a result of this visit and subsequent meetings, a cooperation agreement was signed which had future testing and development of the concept in mind. Bjørn spent close to three months in their development department and ran a team of engineers in the control technology of solenoids.

The result spoke for itself. The speed was increased to more than fifty strokes a second but not without side effects. The noise level being the biggest challenge.

I believe this to be the main reason why Paillard after some time decided to throw in the towel.

At this point several years had gone by since the original idea was conceived and it was not difficult for us to see that new thoughts might lead to far better solutions.

We had meanwhile kept working on several different principles and we were aware that time was about to get away from us as regards the type bar principle.

In our Oslo office hangs to this day a drawing dated the 23.04.1966. Though I've never been a competent drawer, it shows how I at that time pictured a correct future solution to a typing principle.

We were moving into new business challenges and furthermore the so-called servo motor or step motor hadn't been invented yet, which would have been a prerequisite for realizing this idea, so there wasn't much we could have done with the principle at that time; it remained as an idea and a drawing.

Three years later, in 1969, Diablo Data Systems presented the same principle which is clearly illustrated in my drawing. The principle was given the name Daisy Wheel typing principle.

In 1972 the first commercial printer based on this principle was put on the marked and was eventually used in several machines. The speed reached about 30 strokes a second.

Until a new technology replaced this principle at the beginning of the eighties, the Daisy Wheel principle was the dominating one.

From typewriter principles our development path lead into communication systems or so-called Intercom Systems.

Torbjørn got the annual award in 1969 for his industrial design of the world's first fully electronic intercom system which we called "Maxman Electronic". He remained a valuable employee until he retired and was awarded the King's Medal for Long and Faithful Service after forty years in the firm.

With Bjørn as leader of "Research and Development", a lot of pioneering development was made, but that's another exciting story.

As you can see, Reflections and Imagination are not just fancy